There it was. As clear as an autumn sky.

Her stomach clenched, squeezed, made her catch her breath. How could she not have known her own feelings? Love was a huge emotion. She should have been aware of it, should have felt it in her bones, in the very air she breathed.

What now? She loved this wonderful, caring man, and on Saturday she'd have to walk away from him. Again. She couldn't do it.

Dear Reader

Hanmer Springs is a beautiful alpine village set north of Christchurch, in New Zealand's South Island. The hot pools that feature in these pages are a well-known tourist attraction and, for me, very soothing for sore muscles after enduring a gruelling mountain bike race in the region.

I have family living in Hanmer Springs, and on one of my visits there the idea of snow-covered mountains and warm pools intertwined with a love story began to grow. There are many community-minded people living there who have snuck into the background of my story. It is the perfect locale for a specialist children's hospital.

Tom and Fiona are city-dwellers who have both learned to appreciate life away from high-rise buildings and a fast pace of living. But the journey hasn't been easy for either of them, and there is still a long way to go. The past looms large between them, and in Hanmer Springs they find the courage to deal with it. Only then are they able to move forward to the future together they both desired when they were first married eight years earlier.

I hope you enjoy Tom and Fiona's story.

Cheers!

Sue MacKay

THEIR MARRIAGE MIRACLE

BY

SUE MACKAY

First published in Great Britain 2010
Large Print edition 2011
Harlequin Mills & Boon Limited,
Eton House, 18-24 Paradise Road,
Richmond, Surrey TW9 1SR

ISBN: 978 0 263 21733 9

Harlequin Mills & Boon policy is to use papers that are natural, renewable and recyclable products and made from wood grown in sustainable forests. The logging and manufacturing process conform to the legal environmental regulations of the country of origin.

Printed and bound in Great Britain
by CPI Antony Rowe, Chippenham, Wiltshire

With a background working in medical laboratories, and a love of the romance genre, it is no surprise that **Sue MacKay** writes medical romance stories. An avid reader all her life, she wrote her first story at age eight—about a prince, of course. She lives with her husband in beautiful Marlborough Sounds, at the top of New Zealand's South Island, where she can indulge her passions for the outdoors, the sea and cycling. She is currently training as a volunteer ambulance officer.

suemackay.co.nz

For Lindsay and Hannah.
Your unfailing support has been awesome.

CHAPTER ONE

FIONA SAVILLE shivered. It wasn't the unfamiliar ice and snow covering the tiny Hanmer Springs airstrip that sent a chill down her spine, but the battered four-wheel drive approaching along the grass runway. More particularly, the driver of the vehicle.

She leaned back against the Cessna for support. Heaven knew she needed it. Her legs were quivering. *Oh, for goodness' sake, get a grip. You've had ten days to be ready for this.* Her mouth dried. No amount of preparation could have stopped the butterflies now batting around in her stomach. It had been six long, distressing years since she'd last seen Tom.

At least try to look calm. She shoved her shaking hands in her jacket pockets and crossed her ankles. An old pose Tom would recognise as nonchalance. She hoped.

A car skidded to a halt five metres from the tail of the plane and the door cracked open. Fiona's eyes were fixed on the space behind that door, watching the man straightening up as he stepped down on to the ice-encrusted grass.

The ground rolled under her feet. Her shoulder-blades dug into the metal body behind her. Tom looked so—good. So Tom. Lean and tall, strong and loose-limbed, tanned. The door slammed shut, giving her a bigger picture. He was dressed in his usual butt-hugging jeans and open-necked shirt, with the addition of a thick ski jacket. His unruly black curls had fallen prey to a very short cut. Those steely grey eyes held the same alluring temptation she'd once fallen in love with, despite the way they now appeared hard and uncompromising as they focused on her.

A breath trickled through her dry lips. No turning back now. She pushed away from the fuselage and stepped out to face him. 'Hello, Tom. It's good to see you.' If ever there was an understatement that was it. 'I'm glad you came to pick me up and not one of your staff.'

He held her gaze, just for a moment, the tension electric between them. 'Fiona, it's great to see you, too.' He strode across the gap separating them and placed his arms around her in a brief, barely squeezing hug.

She gasped. He smelt the same. That freshly shaven male scent that seemed peculiar to Tom. She jerked away, striving for control over her highly sharpened senses.

'It's been a long while,' he said.

A mental shake and she managed a reply. 'Yes, and I hear you've been busy in that time. Your own specialist children's hospital, no less.'

'We have got a bit to catch up on, haven't we?' He stepped back. 'How was the flight down from Auckland?'

'Moderately turbulent over the Cook Strait and the South Island. There's a storm on the way, due to hit this area late tonight.'

'So I saw on the weather channel. Not unexpected in the middle of winter.' His gaze slid over her, unreadable. 'Thanks for stepping into the breach. I had a mild panic when Jerome had his accident, poor guy. I thought I'd have to cancel the surgery roster for the week.'

He seemed so relaxed, unperturbed at her presence here. How could he be like that after all this time? After the awful way they'd separated? Damn it, but she was about to move into his hospital to work with him and he didn't appear at all flustered.

Take a leaf out of his book. Don't show him the turmoil going on inside. Fiona tugged her shoulders back harder, lifted her chin in an attempt to negate the effect of the flood of anxiety pooling in her stomach, and stretched a smile over her lips.

'It was a bit of luck that I approached the agency when I did.' The medical personnel agency in Auckland had been quick to respond to her initial enquiries about locum work when she returned to New Zealand. Never in a million years would she have expected her first job to be working for Tom.

'I guess it was.'

Was that disappointment lacing his words? Of course he'd have preferred another plastic surgeon to her, but there hadn't been anyone else. 'I'm looking forward to working with you and learning more about your hospital. And to spending some time catching up on what else you've been doing since I left.'

A grimace this time. 'Let's keep everything on a professional level and I'm sure the week will be problem-free.'

'We can't avoid the fact we had a life together.'

He had to have heard the strain in her voice,

but he only said, 'You're right. We can't. But it doesn't have to take over and dominate the reason you are here—which is to perform plastic surgery on my young patients.'

Right, I get the message. She wouldn't avoid trying to broach the past with him—they'd been married after all—but she'd let it go for now. 'Do you come into Theatre to observe the operations done by your specialists?'

'More than that. I assist whenever I can so I know what's going on with each child. And, on a more basic level, it saves me having to employ another surgeon.'

'That's great.' She gulped. Working with Tom this week had just taken on a whole new meaning.

He lifted his sleeve to check his watch. 'Nearly four. We'd better get moving. It'll be dark soon.'

'I need to tie down the plane.' Striding back to the Cessna, Fiona yanked the hatch open and reached inside for the ropes and steel pins required to hold the aircraft on the ground in case the wind got up. So Tom wasn't going to make this week easy. Well, if he thought he could brush her off with a few terse words he'd forgotten just how determined she could be. She wouldn't be leaving until they'd talked about their relationship. It needed sorting out once and for all.

Fiona's heart lurched as she tossed the equipment out. Then again, this week might turn out to be her biggest mistake ever.

Behind her, Tom spoke as though there wasn't any problem. 'I'll do this.'

He reached around her for the mallet, and again that male scent assailed her, stole her voice away so that she couldn't answer him.

Not that he seemed to expect an answer. He began pounding the pegs into the hard earth, adding, 'I still remember the routine.'

So Tom really wasn't at all fazed by her arrival. Shrugging away her disappointment, she reached for her pack, briefcase and laptop, and hauled them across to Tom's vehicle. How long could one week last anyway? Seven days, right? Too long, if the last ten minutes were anything to go by.

She hadn't been expecting Tom to turn up with roses, but she hadn't expected the totally 'let's be professional' bit either. Which just went to show how much she'd deluded herself. She should have known he'd take that stance. It had always been his way of dealing with anything that disturbed him.

How had he reacted when he'd learned that she'd volunteered to take the temporary job? Surely he'd felt something? Anger or warmth? Trepidation or excitement? Maybe he truly didn't care one way or the other. Then again, he'd had days to adjust to the idea. Guilt squeezed her. Six years ago she'd treated him appallingly, leaving as she had. But at the time she hadn't been able to think straight. Through her lawyer she'd made sure he knew she was all right. Hardly the action of a loving wife, but the only way she'd known how to hold on to what remained of her sanity at the time.

She'd often wondered how Tom had dealt with her disappearance. He certainly hadn't broken down any doors looking for her. But had he missed her? Or had he been glad of the quiet, without her there to badger him into talking about the tragedy that had overcome them? Looking at him now, he seemed fine, in control, but he'd always been very good at hiding his feelings. Since she had walked out on him, breaking her marriage vows, he certainly wouldn't trust her on anything these days. Apart from looking after his patients, that was. She'd become very good at plastic surgery, and he'd want the best for his patients, so he'd be prepared to overlook her transgressions of the past for them.

Could he listen to her explanation and forgive her? Let her win his trust back? Only one way to find out, and that did not involve tackling him with a barrage of questions within minutes of seeing him, no matter how hard it was to keep her tongue still.

It had taken her all morning to get up the courage to lift off from Auckland Airport and head this way. But the time had come to clear the air with Tom so she could move forward. Something essential was missing from her life, and she believed that talking to Tom about the past might help to bring final closure so she could stop running away from what had happened.

Apprehension gripped her. What if he clung to keeping the week on a completely professional footing and they never talked about the reasons behind their defunct marriage? That was what she half expected. *So be patient with him.* Huh! If anything would surprise him about her that would, patience having never been her strong point. But the first hurdle of fronting up to him was over. It hadn't been easy. The moment she'd seen him her heart had squeezed with remembered love for this man she'd shared a short marriage with—this man who had been the father of her son.

The man she'd walked out on.

Maybe she needed to forgive herself before expecting Tom to do likewise.

Sliding into the front seat, she hunched her shoulders, not bothering to check that Tom had tied down properly. He'd done it for her often enough in the past to know what he was doing.

But, despite her determination not to watch Tom, her eyes were drawn to him. Did he hold any good memories of her? If so, would they resurface during the next few days? To be so close to Tom after such a long time and not have any real contact could be soul-destroying. From the moment she'd decided to come here she'd known Tom would try to keep her at arm's length. It was up to her to make this work.

The vehicle rocked as Tom climbed in and slammed his door. His seat belt snapped into place. He twisted the ignition key on, but didn't move the gearshift, instead turning to study her.

'You're shivering,' he commented, and flicked on the heater.

'There's a lot of snow out there.' She nodded in the direction of the white and grey mountains dominating the landscape beyond the frozen airfield.

'Guess I'm used to it,' he noted.

'Is that the village?' Fiona pointed through the windscreen. 'Where those lights are at the base of the mountains?'

'Yes. And that's Jack's Pass behind them. It's the road in from the high country farms.'

The whole scene couldn't be any further from where she'd recently been living as it was possible to get. Sand to snow. Roasting temperatures to bone-chilling ice. She tugged her jacket tighter around her. 'Do you like living here?'

'It's where my hospital is.'

'So you moved wherever you had to for the hospital?'

'Basically, yes. But the place has grown on me.' Surprise softened his tight features, as though that idea had only just occurred to him.

'Very different to Auckland.' A city with more than a million people didn't compare to a village of a few hundred.

'More friendly. Even too friendly at times. Everyone likes to know everyone else's business. But there are a lot of pluses to that, too.' Tom still studied her.

What was he looking for? Whatever it was, surely it could wait until they were inside somewhere warm.

'Can we go?' she asked in a quiet voice.

'Sure.' But still he didn't drive off.

Squashing a flare of exasperation, she reached across the seat between them and gripped his arm, shook him. But touching him further unsettled her already stretched nerves. The only man she'd ever loved. Tom. And here she was, unable to ignore those old feelings she'd had for him. Unable to pretend she'd got over him completely.

Snatching her hand back, she wrapped her arms under her breasts as she struggled to control the urgent need to throw herself into his arms and snuggle against his chest. A place she'd always felt safe and loved. If only they could go back in time to when they'd been so happy and in love.

'Fiona? Is there another reason for you coming here?' At last he began driving.

She blinked, dragged her mind together. He'd

dropped the professional approach for a moment. She'd try not to scare him off with her answer.

'I've wanted to catch up with you for a long time, but I haven't had the opportunity to come back to New Zealand for a few years. When I decided to come home on leave I didn't want to have nothing to do, so I put my name down with the medical personnel agency in the hope I'd get work as a locum. When this vacancy was mentioned I jumped at it. I thought I could spend a little time catching up with you while at the same time helping out at your hospital.'

Something deep inside had driven her to come to Hanmer Springs, to Tom. The job was an excuse. She'd have come anyway. She'd loved this man with all her heart, loved him beyond reason. Then she'd gone and treated him appallingly, disappearing out of his life without a backward glace. Now it was time to make amends in some way, if he would let her. If nothing else, she owed him an apology for her behaviour.

Tom's hands gripped the steering wheel, making his driving stiff and jerky. 'Don't expect too much of my time, Fiona. We are a very busy hospital.'

She said softly, 'I'm very glad I can help out.'

The butterflies tripping around her stomach became thundering elephants as her mind refused to consider how she'd survive the coming days if Tom didn't spend some personal time with her. Though she still believed she'd done the right thing in coming to help, so that Tom's young patients didn't have to suffer long delays for their surgery, only now did she understand how high the cost of spending a full week around Tom could be to herself. Enormous, if she wasn't careful to keep her emotions under some sort of control. The love she'd felt for Tom might not have survived, but there were still a lot of feelings for him that hadn't gone away and which she wasn't prepared to face. The sense of belonging with him, the old need to always tell him everything, the longing for the solidarity she'd known with him. Those were the rocks their marriage had been built on—the things she'd missed as much as his love.

'We'd better get a move on. Some of your patients have already arrived, and they're anxious to meet you.' He braked for the narrow gateway out on to the gravel road.

'Is anyone concerned about the change of surgeon?'

'Some parents are a little apprehensive, but that's probably due to nerves about their children undergoing surgery.' He hesitated. 'You've got a lot to do this week. Wait until you see the stack of patient files on your desk.'

'I've seen the surgical roster. Not a lot of time to spare.' Not a lot of time to get alongside Tom. But she was here, in his village, about to work at his hospital, prepared to give him everything she had to assuage her guilt. That was a start. Then all she had to do was get him to understand that she'd left him for his own good.

That was all. She flicked her middle finger with her thumb. Might as well climb Mount Everest without an oxygen tank on her back.

Tom gave her his first full-blown smile. 'Think of all the children you'll be helping by making their worlds a happier place.'

It seemed crazy that an irrational jag of joy should strike her at the sight of that heart-melting smile, but she saw it as progress. One teeny step forward. His patients were the way through his barriers. 'If I can fix things for any child then I'm very pleased to do so.'

And if she could fix what was wrong between

her and Tom, then so much the better. Then she'd be able to get on with deciding what was the next phase in her life.

CHAPTER TWO

IT FELT weird to be sitting beside Tom as he drove them to the hospital. Strangely, Fiona felt as though the intervening years apart hadn't happened. Yet she didn't know what to say, how to make ordinary conversation.

During the short trip past alpine chalets lining the village streets Fiona felt her muscles tighten more with every minute she sat beside a now silent Tom. She wondered what he was thinking about. His rigid back and tense shoulders were a bit of a clue that he felt strange in this situation too. Gone were any remnants of that earlier smile.

Perhaps small talk would lighten the atmosphere. 'Tom—'

'Fiona—'

'You first.'

'After you,' Tom muttered as he turned into a wide, tree-lined driveway and braked.

Her mouth fell open at her first glimpse of

Tom's hospital. Surprise rocketed through her, all thought of what she'd been about to say forgotten.

'Welcome to the Specialist Children's Hospital.'

'Wow. It's impressive. And gorgeous.' An enormous brick dwelling dominated extensive well-groomed lawns. It was three storeys high and shaped like a square C, and ivy covered the majority of the old, darkened brick exterior.

'Isn't it?' His tone softened, as did his taut muscles. Pride made his eyes sparkle.

'I expected something new and utilitarian, but this looks like those mansions you see in English country magazines. How did you find it?' When she'd left they'd been living in Auckland, hundreds of kilometres away in the North Island.

'It belonged to the parents of a colleague. They'd lived here most of their married life, brought their family up here, but when it was time to move into a retirement village they were reluctant to sell. The idea of a place for children to come and heal excited them to the point that they negotiated a very good price with me.'

'It still must have cost a fortune.'

'It did.'

It did. That was all he had to say. She recognised

a stop sign when she saw one. True, it wasn't any of her business, but her interest was well and truly piqued. Tom had created something special here—something that she hadn't even known he'd wanted to do. Had she been so self-absorbed that she hadn't heard him talk about his dreams? He'd become a brilliant paediatrician, and she'd supposed that was enough for him.

'You've created something tangible, something that says *This is what I do, who I am.* It's wonderful.' Using these bricks and mortar he'd formed the basis of his future, whereas she'd led a nomadic life, moving from post to post as required. Her work had been no less important, but poles apart from his. Which said a lot about them as a couple. Had they always been destined to go in opposite directions? Odd when they both had the same goal at heart—to help people, and more particularly children.

The look he sent her suggested she'd let her tongue get carried away. But he did answer. 'I like stability.'

And she'd wrecked that for him. But he'd obviously recovered enough to regain it. Tom would always live here, while she didn't have a clue where she'd be ten weeks from now. He'd know what would be happening for the foreseeable future while all she knew was that she'd be performing plastic surgery. That could happen anywhere in the world.

Her eyes were drawn back to the hospital. In the cold, grey dusk the building was imposing. Where had the money come from? While at med school Tom had taken any job wherever possible to pay his way, and his parents had struggled to help him as much as they could. Even after he'd qualified and paid off his student loans—which he hadn't let her help him with—he wouldn't have amassed the sort of money required to buy this place. Even at a discounted price.

She said, 'I could've helped financially if I'd known.' If he'd told her.

'No, Fiona, you couldn't have. It worked better for me this way.'

Of course Tom hadn't wanted her help. This was his project, and her money would have taken something else away from him. She'd already made one big mistake in their lives; he wouldn't trust her not to make another.

'I think I understand.'

'Do you?'

She nodded. 'After the years I've just spent

living a life based entirely on my own abilities and not what my father's wealth could buy me, I do understood what it means to achieve something on your own merits.'

His eyebrows rose. 'You're being harsh on yourself. No one else could make you into the surgeon you've become. You did that yourself.'

'Thanks, but something like this is different. This is huge.' A warm glow settled over her. Tom had given her a small compliment. She'd treasure it.

He didn't know that she'd learned to give so much more of herself to other people than she'd ever done before. In the process she'd found that she got back truckloads more than she could ever have believed possible, often in the most unexpected and quite beautiful ways. Like the little Pakistani girl's parents, who'd given her the family chickens as repayment for reconstructing the child's badly burned face. She'd cried when they'd brought in the birds, their livelihood, and she'd had to dig deep to find an acceptable reason that wouldn't offend the parents when she'd asked them to keep the fowls. She smiled at the memory, and again focused on the building.

'How long have you owned the property?'

'Nearly five years.' Tom explained, 'Andy set up a trust and raised an unbelievably huge amount of money. Not just to buy the building, but to help keep the place running.' He shook his head. 'I'm still not sure how he managed it, but it was above board and that's all that bothered me.'

'Andy? As in Andrew?' The entrepreneur of Tom's family, Andrew had got on well with her father. Sometimes she'd wondered if her father thought she'd married the wrong brother.

'He's done extremely well for himself over the years.'

'It seems you have too.' Despite everything that had happened to Tom, it seemed he'd managed to get his life back on track. 'I'm really glad for you.'

'Thanks.'

'Just because our marriage didn't work out doesn't mean I don't want happiness for you. Or at least a life that fulfils you.'

'It's full, that's for sure.' Tom gazed around at the immaculate lawns with oak trees lining the perimeter.

But not fulfilled? She wondered about that. She hoped he was happy, while at the same time the thought made her feel even more unsettled about her own future. *Get over yourself. Don't start the 'what ifs'.*

'When did the hospital become operational?' she asked. It was a bit awkward getting a conversation flowing, but she'd persevere.

'My first patient walked through the front door a little over three years ago.'

'It must have been exciting.' She wished she'd been here to see it, to share that moment with Tom. Another thing lost because of her stupidity.

'Incredibly so.' His fingers drummed the steering wheel. 'Well worth all the hard work. There were months when I didn't believe I'd ever see the day this became a fully functioning hospital and not just a dream.'

'You weren't working?'

'Full-time in the paediatric unit at Christchurch Hospital, which is about an hour and a half from here. Close enough to be harassed by builders and tradesmen, but too far to make the travelling back and forth easy.'

'That sounds exhausting.' But he'd have managed. This was a man who always focused completely on work, often to the detriment of everything else. Setting up a new facility would have just been another job to see through to the end.

'Very.'

'I read an article in a medical journal about the work you're doing with children and their families coping with chronic diseases. Spending a week here with other similarly afflicted children must have huge benefits for the kids involved. Also for their parents. Getting together with other parents to share experiences must be a tremendous help. You're earning a superb reputation amongst your peers.'

'We're booked up solid for the next six months.'

'That's a lot of children you're helping.' Tenderness for him slid softly through her. Helping children was what made him tick. And, if he was anything like her since Liam's death, saving people would have become the prime focus of his life. But he didn't know about the long, hard years she'd spent working with people in dreadful situations. 'I think what you're doing is absolutely wonderful. I'm looking forward to you showing me around.'

Tom stared at her for a long moment. What did he see? The woman she'd become? The pain in the backside she'd used to be? More importantly, would he give her a chance to explain herself? Show him how different she was these days? It suddenly became important that he got to know her again. Then he might begin to see her for the selfless woman she'd become, and not the lost and helpless creature who'd left him. Or the extravagant, spoilt girl he'd first met.

'You'll get the tour. Everyone does.' He looked away, slid the vehicle into gear and drove forward. 'Did you receive the case notes my secretary prepared for tomorrow's operating schedule?'

Back to business. She swallowed her disappointment. 'Yes, they came through late yesterday. I've read them thoroughly, and I'll be taking another look through each one later tonight after I've seen my patients. I've read enough to answer any worries they or their parents may have. I'd also like to see where I'll be working before tomorrow, if that's possible.'

'Of course.'

A young woman in a nurse's uniform closed in on Tom as he stepped down from the vehicle. 'Tom, thank goodness you're back. Jarrod Harris fell out of a tree just after you left for the airstrip. He's broken his arm.'

'What was he doing climbing a tree?' Even as Tom asked, he began striding towards the hospital.

Fiona followed quickly, almost trotting to keep up as Tom's long legs stretched out, eating up the ground in his hurry to see his patient. And get away from her?

'Who's Jarrod Harris?' she asked.

'One of a group of haemophiliac patients staying this week for mentoring, friendship and medical talks,' Tom explained, before asking the other woman, 'Where's everyone?'

'Kerry's with Jarrod. The interns went into the village earlier, to pick up a prescription for one of the children at the pharmacy and then on for a coffee. I haven't called them as I knew you'd be back any moment.'

Tom slowed his pace enough to allow Fiona to catch up for introductions. 'Stella, this is Fiona Sav—Fraser, the plastic surgeon.'

Fiona saw him blink, nearly trip, when he realised he'd been about to use her married name. She hadn't gone back to her maiden name, but of course Tom had presumed so. She stared back, trying not to succumb to the wave of anguish spreading through her, bringing an ache in the region of her heart.

She said, 'Actually, my name's still Saville.'

It had never crossed her mind to change back

to Fraser. That would have been another bond between them broken. It wasn't as though she'd ever regretted marrying Tom.

He swallowed, then turned to the other woman staring at them both with curiosity scrunching her face. 'Fiona is my ex-wife.'

Stella gaped. 'I didn't know you were divorced.'

'I'm—we're not.'

But they'd be getting around to it very soon, Fiona guessed by the startled look in Tom's eyes. It made perfect sense now that they'd caught up with each other. Why did she feel so sad? Their marriage was long over. *But I don't want a divorce.* Which begged the question, what did she want? Her thumb flicked her forefinger. Her heart thumped under her ribs. *Definitely not.*

Tom continued, oblivious to her feelings, 'Stella's our head theatre nurse. If you need to know anything, ask her.'

'Hello, Stella. I guess that means we'll be working together this week.'

'Yes, we will.' The nurse glanced sideways at her, a multitude of questions racing across her face.

Those questions brought another thought to mind. Had Tom settled down with another woman? Six years was a long time to remain single, especially for a warm, caring man like Tom. Women had always been attracted to him, so it wouldn't have been hard for him to find someone else. Her heart squeezed tight. Of course she didn't mind. She would be very happy for him if that was the case. Really. Her hands clenched at her sides. Really.

'Jarrod's in the recovery room.' Stella broke through Fiona's tumultuous thoughts.

Tom fired questions at his nurse. 'Any other injuries? Did he knock his head? Lose consciousness? There'll probably be internal bleeding from landing on the ground.'

'He's got a few scratches with light bleeding and says he didn't hit his head. He seems remarkably happy, as though he's done nothing wrong climbing that tree.' Stella's lips tightened with disapproval.

Fiona followed Tom into the theatre recovery room. A boy of about ten years lay on the bed. A light smattering of blood, which appeared to have come from a deep scratch on his hand, stained his denim jacket and jeans. A woman holding a penlight torch peered under his eyelids.

'Kerry, thanks for coming in. Any major

problems with our lad?' Tom asked, reaching for an X-ray film lying on the end of the bed.

'Apart from a broken arm, he's a very lucky boy. His vitals are good, shock level low.'

The boy grinned, before wincing as pain snagged him. 'It wasn't a big tree.'

'You shouldn't have been up it at all,' Tom growled. But understanding lightened his face as he put aside the X-ray to gently palpate Jarrod's lower left arm.

Tom looked to Fiona. 'Looks like our tour is on hold.' He nodded to the woman with the penlight. 'Kerry's one of our anaesthetists. Kerry, this is Fiona Fraser, the plastic surgeon.'

And he was sticking to using her maiden name. Pain stabbed her beneath the ribs as she reached for Kerry's outstretched hand.

'I'm glad we've caught up before we start tomorrow's surgery.'

Kerry's dazzling smile made Fiona feel welcome for the first time since she'd touched down on the airstrip. The hard knot in her stomach finally eased a little. 'So am I.'

Stella spoke to Tom. 'I'm sorry, but I can't stay. I've got to prepare for my in-laws' wedding anniversary dinner.'

Tom waved at her. 'I'm sorry, I'd forgotten all about you wanting to leave early. You get going. We'll manage here.'

'I can help you with Jarrod,' Fiona offered, watching Stella leave and thinking how different Tom's attitude had become. He'd always used to expect his staff to put patients before everything. 'I've worked with a lot of children recently,' she added defensively.

Tom glanced up, an assessing look in those steely eyes. Then he dipped his chin. 'Jumping straight in? Why not? I'd appreciate it. The haemophilia might mean this is not a straight-forward fracture.'

Warmth spread through her at the thought of working with Tom again. Then Jarrod groaned, quickly dampening her mood. She queried Tom, 'Have you got clotting factors on hand? Vitamin K?'

'Plenty of those. With eight haemophiliacs here this week, we're well prepared.' Tom lifted his head from examining Jarrod and focused on Fiona. 'We'll set this fracture, clean up that cut and those scratches, then a shot of vitamin K and some clotting factor to stop the bleeding.'

'Haemophilia A or B?' she asked.

'A, but I'd still like to check his notes.'

But he knew what was in those notes, which went to show how thoroughly he worked with each patient.

'Here you go.' Kerry handed a file over to Tom. 'Do you need me for anything else? If not I'd like to get back to the twins. We were in the middle of baths when Stella phoned.'

'Twins? How old are they?' Fiona turned to the anaesthetist.

'Three-year-old rascals.'

'You must have your hands full at times.' Fiona pushed down on a sudden spurt of longing to hold a small child. Often, especially after she'd spent time at one of the clinics where she worked, this need would overtake her, rattle her, and keep her awake at nights. But why right now, when she was with Tom for the first time in years? It wasn't as though she would ever be having another child. And certainly not with Tom. But she had had a baby, a beautiful little boy, and here she stood beside his father, totally confused, ready to run and hide from all the emotion assailing her.

Kerry spoke as though from far away. 'They keep us very busy, the adorable scallywags.'

Huh? What? Of course, the twins. Concentrate.

On answering Kerry. On helping Jarrod. As if she could control her emotions that easily. But she had to. Her smile stretched her lips tight. 'How do you manage to work as well as look after two children? Do you have a nanny?'

'I only work every second week, and my sister-in-law looks after them for me those days.'

Tom waved a hand in Kerry's direction. 'Get out of here while you can. And give those two bundles of trouble a hug from their godfather.'

'Come and do that yourself. If they don't see you soon they'll think you're a stranger next time you arrive bearing armloads of gifts. And bring Fiona with you.'

Godfather? Tom? He'd be fantastic. He adored children, and seemed to know instinctively how to communicate with them at any age. Another familiar pain curled around her heart, stopping her from moving. Her head filled with the vision of Tom holding his dark-haired son in his arms and rocking him to sleep with infinite patience; and the old pain that she'd learned to breathe through, live through, but never to vanquish, seized her. Tom should have more children of his own. He was missing out on so much. So were those unborn babies.

Her eyes fluttered shut as she struggled to rein in her seesawing emotions. Meeting up with Tom again was turbulent. And with past issues already battering at her in a way she hadn't expected she felt bruised internally. She leaned into the wall for a moment, gathering her strength.

'Fi? Are you all right?' A strong hand held her elbow with surprising gentleness.

Sweet mama, please don't call me Fi. Fi belonged to another time, another life. A life when this man had loved her. 'Yes, I'm fine. I don't know what came over me.'

When she opened her eyes again she found Tom watching her closely. She dragged out a smile. 'Where do you keep the clotting factors? I'll get them for you.'

His hand stayed on her elbow, sending heat up her arm. Her body leaned closer to him. 'Are you ill?' he asked softly.

'Not at all. Just a bit tired, I guess. It was a long flight and I'm out of practice.'

'Keep Jarrod entertained for a few minutes while I fetch his shots. Then I'll take you to get a cup of tea and some food. I bet you haven't eaten in hours. Do you still get light-headed and cranky when you're hungry?' His lips curved ever so slightly upward.

'Not normally.' But today hadn't been exactly normal.

'Then I'm a lot safer already.'

Was he teasing her?

Fiona shook her head as he headed out the room. If Tom could find it in himself to tease her then things might be looking up.

He returned quickly, with a stainless steel dish containing vials and a syringe. 'Okay, young man. Let's get this over.'

Jarrod held an arm out, heavily scarred from numerous similar injections. 'Bang it in there, Doc.'

As Tom filled the syringe with vitamin K, he spoke to Jarrod. 'Tell me why you were climbing a tree in icy conditions.'

'Because it's fun.' Jarrod's lips squeezed together and his eyes were slits, daring Tom to disagree with him.

Fiona grinned. 'Of course it is. Trees are made for boys to climb.'

'See!' Jarrod's eyes lit up as he faced off Tom. 'She understands, and she's not a boy.'

Tom shoved his hand across his scalp in a

gesture so familiar Fiona's stomach knotted. Except in the past his hair had been a tangle of curls. 'I guess I have to agree about the fun.'

'Girls like climbing trees, too. But you still have to be careful, Jarrod,' Fiona admonished gently.

'Yeah, I know, but I wanted to go higher than the others.'

'And now you've got a broken arm. No doubt you're in some pain as well,' Tom noted.

'It does hurt.' Jarrod winced. 'But it's worth it. This is a cool place, and I've got new friends.'

'That's what this week's all about,' Tom smiled at the boy, genuine warmth lightening his eyes. Then he turned to her. 'When did you last plaster an arm?'

'Probably when I was an intern.' Was this a small olive branch? Working together on Jarrod's arm?

Tom manoeuvred Jarrod through the door and into a smaller room. 'What do you reckon, Jarrod? Should we let Dr Fraser loose on you?'

'Yeah. Can I write on the arm so she gets the right one?' Jarrod dragged up a cheeky grin, but his pale cheeks showed he was tiring.

'How about I plaster your mouth and keep you quiet for a while?' Fiona winked at the boy.

'Mum would love that.'

'Okay, let's get this done. Fiona, I'll hold the arm if you want to start.' Tom nodded to the tape waiting on a bench-top.

Jarrod's arm was soon in a cast and resting in a sling.

'You be careful with that, young man.' Tom sounded stern. 'Don't go hitting any of your new mates over their heads with it. I don't want to find I'm stitching up skull wounds all week.'

Fiona grinned. Her tension had slipped away while they'd worked together. It felt good. There might be a lot of misunderstanding between them, but at least they were on the same side when it came to their patient. And they'd communicated without words as she'd wound the wet tape around Jarrod's arm. So, they hadn't lost everything that had been good between them. But was it enough to find their way back to a point where they could really discuss the past and lay it to rest for ever?

Tom explained everything to Jarrod's parents when they arrived moments later, anxious and dishevelled. After hugs and affectionate growls at their son, they led a chastened Jarrod away to his room, and Tom turned to Fiona.

'Come on. I'll show you your accommodation. Then we can grab that cup of tea before your first appointment.' He slung her pack over his shoulder and took her elbow. Instantly he knew he'd made a mistake. To hold her, no matter how lightly, zapped his brain, befuddled him completely. But she'd looked so lost that he'd had to take hold of her and lead her along. He'd acted without thought. The desire to help her was an integral part of him and had been from the day he'd first set eyes on her in the paediatric ward of Auckland Hospital.

He kept his hand on her elbow. He could still be professional and hold her like this. *Yeah, right.* So much for his self-control.

'The tea sounds wonderful,' Fiona murmured.

Her honeyed voice sent memories clawing through his mind. Memories that slammed through his body and lifted goosebumps on his skin. Memories that dredged up confusion and nostalgia. Heat and fire.

His reaction to her shocked him. He'd schooled

his mind to accept her coming to Hanmer Springs. He hadn't thought it would be too hard to keep her at arm's length. He'd tried to convince himself that he was so over her that she could dance naked in front of him and he'd turn away.

'Liar.' He'd never be able to do that.

'What?' Fiona asked.

'You caught me talking to myself.' He'd made a mistake earlier when he'd called her Fi. His stomach clenched in a spasm. *Don't start thinking of her as Fi.* That was a sure-fire way of getting entangled in emotions he didn't want to face. He had loved her deeply, and some of those feelings still existed, pulling him to her even as he grappled with her presence. Did she know how shaken he felt by her appearance? He desperately hoped not. She must not know she still had the power to unnerve him. Ever since he'd learned that Jerome's replacement was none other than Fiona he'd felt antsy, as if something he didn't want to deal with was about to slap him across the face, and if anyone could make him face up to whatever that was, Fiona could.

He headed out into the corridor and strove for a neutral subject to talk about. 'I take it from what you said you haven't done much flying lately?'

'I've kept current, but that's about all. Hiring a plane isn't always easy in some of the countries I've been to.' She shivered, as though she had a chill, and hugged herself tight.

'Look at you. You're freezing.' The building felt very snug to him. 'We've got heat pumps everywhere.'

Her eyes rolled. 'It's not exactly the middle of summer in here.'

'How long have you been back from Pakistan?' He still had trouble believing she'd worked there. But according to her CV that wasn't the only part of the world she'd been to.

'I spent nearly a month in Australia with Dad, then came home a few days ago.'

'All that heat? Those flies? I am finding it hard to imagine you in those conditions.'

That stung her. He saw it in the clenching of her hands, in the widening of her eyes and the tightening of her mouth. Unwittingly he'd insulted her.

Remorse mingled with curiosity within him. 'I'm sorry. I didn't mean to sound so rude. I seem to be overreacting to everything you say.'

Her reply was quiet, thoughtful. 'I can understand your sentiments. I'd have said the same thing a few years ago, but believe it or not, I've changed.' She hesitated, as though wondering how much to say.

'Tell me more.' He found he really did want to know all about her, and not because he needed the distraction. Where had she spent the years since they'd separated? Who had she worked for? How had she coped with her grief?

Her chin lifted and her shoulders tugged back, in that endearing manner of hers. 'You've seen my credentials. I've worked in various countries where people have nothing but a tin roof over their heads. Mostly doing skin grafts over burns, repairing scars—anything to make their lives a little less horrific.'

'Fi, it's fantastic, but you have to admit you had no intention of doing anything like that when you were still specialising.' Damn it, he'd used the Fi word again. But again she'd surprised him. Leopards didn't change their spots. Neither would Fiona go to live in some of the most uncomfortable locations in the world. Not unless she took a jumbo jet full of luxuries to keep her happy.

Wait up. He wasn't giving her a chance. Already he'd noticed small changes in her. Mostly physical ones, true. And in the kind of clothes she now wore. She also seemed a lot calmer than she'd used to be. So what was to say she hadn't changed majorly in her attitude to life? She'd certainly had plenty of reasons to. If she had, he could only admire her for it. And wonder where she was emotionally. Had she got over Liam's death enough to want children again? Had she managed to get to the point where she could look back on their marriage and remember the good things it had had going for it?

He remembered a lot of those good things, but that didn't mean he wanted to repeat the experience. Friday nights had been especially lonely ever since she'd left, because Fiona had always made them special—closing out the world, tuning out work, cooking a meal that they had time to enjoy while they chatted and relaxed and laughed together. He'd missed her spontaneous hugs and the way she'd creep up behind him to slide her arms around his waist and lay her face on his back between his shoulder blades. That small act had always made him feel so loved. He shoved down on the knot of warmth creeping under his ribs and changed tack.

'What happened to that fantastic opportunity to go into private practice with some of the country's best plastic surgeons waiting for you once you'd qualified?'

'I turned it down. It didn't seem like the right thing for me any more. And as it happened, it was the best decision career-wise I ever made.' As she talked her deep azure eyes lightened—eyes that had haunted his sleep for six long, unrelenting years.

Glancing at his watch, he told her, 'I'd like to hear all about what you've been up to, but it'll have to wait. Time's speeding by.' He strode along the corridor to the staff quarters and the door leading out to his cottage. He wanted to pretend she wasn't right behind him. He needed space between them so he could put everything back into perspective. *Fat chance.* Hearing her trotting steps as her shorter legs tried to keep pace with his long ones made him smile inside, and he slowed down to accommodate her, as he'd used to before they'd crashed and burned.

'Fi—' *Damn it.* 'Fiona, let me take those other bags.' He reached for them, slipping them out of her grasp.

'I can manage.'

'I know, but humour me. I'm trying to be the perfect host.'

She smiled up at him, and his heart lurched. Just like that. A simple smile, and she'd tugged him even closer, had him remembering all sorts of sweet things about her.

Whoa. Go carefully. Put the barriers back up and keep your distance. Because, as much as he felt drawn to Fiona again, he couldn't trust her not to trample on his feelings. In order to protect himself he had to remember to act professionally with her.

CHAPTER THREE

FIONA missed Tom's hand on her elbow the moment he reached for her other bags. If it had meant carrying her bags to keep that small contact then she'd have gladly done so. But she didn't have a choice.

So she'd try talking instead.

'Tell me how it works around here. Where your patients come from, that sort of thing.'

'There are two components to the hospital.' Relief underlined Tom's words, as though he might be grateful for the change in topic. 'The surgical unit where you'll be working is where we see children from all over the South Island who need various specialists' care. I look after the general paediatric cases. Then I get in other specialists, usually for a week at a time.'

'So this week is devoted to patients requiring plastic surgery?'

'Exactly. A lot of the children are from underprivileged backgrounds, but I take everyone who needs us and find funding from various sources.'

'Social Services?'

'For some cases. We also rely on charities. In here.' He waved her into a large room containing a kitchen and dining area at one end, an array of comfortable armchairs and a television at the other. 'This is the communal living quarters used by specialist staff we draft in and the interns who rotate through here from Canterbury Medical School.'

He paused to draw a deep breath, and Fiona instantly sensed she wasn't going to like what he was about to say.

'All the rooms are in use, so originally I arranged for Jerome to share my cottage. We get on very well and have become friends over the years.' His troubled gaze met hers with defiance. 'Which means you are now sharing with me. I know it's not going to be easy for either of us, but I hope we can make it work.'

'You couldn't change the arrangements?' She couldn't blame him if he'd wanted to, but nor could she stop the hurt that stabbed her.

'Unfortunately not—because that would've

been for the best.' His tone was neutral, but his stance rigid.

'I'm not here for an argument, Tom. I'm filling a gap at the hospital for you.' Exasperation rocked through her. Her bottom lip trembled. Exhaustion had caught up, big-time. What else could be causing this reaction to him? Certainly not having him standing so close to her.

Moving away, she stared at up at his face, suddenly cross for putting them both in this situation. Drawing a deep breath—a steady one, she was surprised to note—she suggested, 'How about I move into a motel or hotel in the village? It's only half a kilometre away. I won't need transport and I'd be available all the time.'

'I already tried that but everything's booked out. There's a golf tournament on this week. Plus it's school holidays, and many families come here for the snow and hot pools.'

'Guess we're stuck with this arrangement, then.'

Tom mightn't be too happy about it, but she felt another surge of hope. This could be the opportunity that she wanted to get alongside him again. But first she'd let him get used to having her around.

'I'll do my best to stay out of your way. Now, where's this place you live? I'd like to unpack and put on some warmer clothes.'

Tom stood looking at her as though he had more to say. But finally he turned around, wrenched open an outside door, and led the way along a path winding to a stone cottage set amongst young oak trees.

'Here's a key for you.' He delved into his pocket. 'Come and go as you please.'

'Is there anyone else living here?' Did he have a partner she needed to know about? 'Am I going to get in anyone else's way in the bathroom?' Her stomach crunched as she waited for his reply.

His grey eyes darkened with sadness. 'I live alone. And, for the record, I haven't got a woman in my life at the moment.'

'I find that hard to believe.' She smiled, and her stomach relaxed. Why did this knowledge make her feel better? It wasn't as though she'd come to claim Tom back. Something niggled at the back of her brain. Really? No, this week was about tying up the loose ends, not starting over.

'I'm not saying I haven't dated on and off, but this place takes up a lot of my attention. No one

I've met has been able to deal with that. I guess I'm too selfish to make allowances.'

'I'd say you were dedicated.' And still working every hour there was in a day, to the detriment of everything else.

'What about you? Have you taken any poor, unsuspecting man to meet your father over the years?' A straightforward question, but did she hear more than curiosity behind the words?

'No way.' Then a chuckle tripped over her tongue at the memory of Tom meeting her father for the first time. 'I'm not game enough to put anyone through that ordeal ever again.'

He nodded, gave an exaggerated shudder. 'Very wise. Meeting your father is not to be taken lightly, or without protection.'

She grinned, remembering the difficult introduction Tom and her father had had. From that day on they'd never agreed on anything. They'd both loved her for different reasons and in different ways. Her father had demanded too much of her. Her husband had asked nothing of her. 'Believe it or not, Dad's calmed down a lot lately, having finally accepted that I will live my life how I want to, not how he expects. And I've learned not to try and live up to his expectations.'

'Bet that wasn't easy.' A twinkle lightened his eyes. 'Let's go in before you freeze to death.'

Inside the front door, Fiona stared around the tiny entranceway and along the hall, avidly looking for anything from their life together. All she saw were stunning black and white landscapes: mountains, rivers, the ocean.

'Your photography is still superb.'

'The scenery around here lends itself to great photographs.'

She quickly scanned the photos, searching. Not one photo of the two of them. Nothing of Liam. As a keen photographer, Tom used to plaster the walls of their home with photos. Many of her, she admitted. Her mood slumped. She had been expecting too much. Disappointment stabbed her diaphragm, as though she had a stitch from running too hard. Putting a hand to the wall, she leaned against it, sucking air through her teeth.

Her pack landed with a thud on the floor of a room off to the left, and Tom called out, 'This is your room. Mine's opposite, while the kitchen, lounge and bathroom are at the end of the hall.'

With an effort, she dragged herself upright and clumped through the bedroom door. The furnishings in the small, neat room were sparse. The bed stood square to the wall, the coverings tucked in evenly. Only the vibrant terracotta and blue decorating made the room warm and welcoming. Tom had a good eye for colour.

'This will be fine.' It was luxury after Pakistan. Then she thought about the time she'd just spent in Sydney with her father on her way home. His new apartment overlooking Sydney Harbour was crammed with luxuries. What she'd once taken for granted now seemed obscenely excessive. This small room was perfect.

'The kitchen's well stocked, so help yourself to anything you want. There's a firebox that runs day and night. You'll soon feel warmer.'

Her body might feel warmer, but she doubted her heart would ever defrost. It had frozen all those years ago and she'd never known how to thaw it. She'd tried talking with Tom then, but she hadn't been able to find the right words to get through to him. The harder she'd tried, the worse she'd made things and the further away from her he'd pulled, until they hadn't been able to talk about anything. Not even what to have for breakfast.

Tom's voice broke through her reverie. 'Do you still take milk in your tea?'

A mundane question that spoke of a past they'd shared and hinted that now there might be things neither knew about each other.

'Definitely no milk. I got used to drinking black tea while travelling.'

Again those eyebrows rose in astonishment, but at least his eyes were on the friendly side of the barometer. 'As I said, I'm looking forward to hearing about your excursions.'

'You're still finding it hard to believe I could leave my feather duvet behind?'

'Do you blame me?'

No, she couldn't. Sometimes it had been hard enough believing it herself.

Tom stretched his legs out under his desk and yawned. 'Sorry, late night last night.'

Fiona was with him in his consulting room, meeting the patients on tomorrow's operating schedule. He'd sat quietly throughout each consultation, listening and observing. Now she'd just finished talking to the parents of a six-month-old baby born with a cleft palate, hopefully allaying their fears about their darling child undergoing surgery. She always felt a small thrill at being able to repair the fissure in a baby's mouth, making that child's life normal and saving them terrible angst as they grew up and mixed with more and more people.

'A patient keep you up?' she asked. Or one of those women who couldn't deal with his dedication to his hospital? Fiona wondered.

Snap out of it. The guy had a life, and he didn't have to explain himself to her. If his life appeared a whole lot more balanced than hers, then she'd be pleased for him. It wasn't his fault hers lacked love and friendship. She'd made it that way. Deliberately. In an attempt to keep it pain-free.

'No, a birthday party for one of the staff. Hanmer Springs isn't as dull as some people would have you think.' Tom smiled. 'Though it does take some getting used to. At least it did for me, being a city dweller. There's excitement, and then there's excitement.'

She grinned straight back. 'Late nights never used to wear you out. You showing your age, or what?' Clapping her hand against her forehead, she exclaimed, 'Oh, of course—it's the big four O coming up at the end of this year. No wonder you're so tired, you old man.'

'Careful, you're only five years behind me.'

He looked darned good, having matured from the boyish good-looks of the thirty-year-old she'd first met into a very handsome man comfortable in his own skin. Even the new lines around his mouth added character.

'That's a lifetime, buster,' she quipped, before concentrating on the pages in her hand, needing to quell the sudden thumping in her chest. 'There are some notes on a boy here that I didn't receive by fax. Cameron Gordon?'

'A late addition to tomorrow's list. The paperwork arrived in this morning's post. He had a cleft palate repaired when he was a baby but for some reason his harelip wasn't corrected.'

'But he's ten. He must've suffered a lot of teasing over the years.'

'I think he got lost in the system. His parents divorced when he was three, and from what I can gather he's been shunted back and forth between them ever since. When his GP phoned on Wednesday asking me to help I couldn't refuse.'

'Do you ever turn a child away?'

Tom shrugged. 'Not if I can help it.'

A gentle tap on the door interrupted them.

'Sophie Clark and her father are here,' the

cheerful receptionist announced, and held the door wider to allow them through.

Fiona uncrossed her ankles and straightened up from leaning against the edge of Tom's desk, then turned to greet her last patient.

A middle-aged man gently led a slight, shy teen-age girl into the room. The girl hunched against her father, her face hidden behind a curtain of long hair.

Fiona's heart went out to this girl, who obviously hated people seeing her damaged face. A jolt of sadness hit Fiona when she saw the jagged purple scar marring Sophie's left cheek from just below the eye to the corner of her mouth. The medical notes mentioned a car accident.

Tom shook Mr. Clark's hand, saying, 'Jacob, good to see you again. Sophie, how are you? How did you do in the school's short story contest?'

'I won.' Sophie smiled, the dullness in her eyes lifting. She was a beautiful girl, with fine bone structure and enormous eyes, and eyelashes that had to be the envy of every female alive.

'Brilliant.' Tom clapped his hands. 'Now, take a seat. This is Dr Fraser.'

'Hi, Sophie. I'm your specialist this week.'

'Hello, Dr Fraser.'

'Call me Fiona. It's easier.' And she was not used to being called Dr Fraser.

Sophie turned the left side of her face away again. 'Okay, Fiona.'

Fiona sat opposite the girl and reached for her hand. 'Sophie, you're a very beautiful girl, and what's happened to your face doesn't change that.'

Scepticism clouded Sophie's face, and her shoulders tensed. 'Yeah, right.'

'I mean it. You have the sort of strong bone structure that most women would give anything to have.' Reaching for the hand mirror she'd placed on Tom's desk earlier, Fiona tentatively held it up in front of Sophie. Then she leaned over to run a fingertip across the girl's right cheekbone. 'See how high your cheekbones are?' she asked, in a soft, but determined tone.

Sophie darted a glance at the mirror, looked away, despair filling her eyes, tears welling up.

'And your skin—it's so clear of blemishes. How do you manage to avoid pimples at your age?'

'Guess I got lucky with something.' Sophie shrugged. 'But no one wants to look at me now. I'm ugly. You don't know what it's like.'

'You're right, I don't.' Fiona cringed at the

anguish this young woman suffered. 'But I know you're not ugly. Forget that idea. Let's really look at you. Take the mirror while I show you the real Sophie Clark.'

Fiona held her breath as she waited for the girl's response. No one in the room moved. Then, just as Fiona sensed Tom about to intervene, Sophie snatched the mirror out of Fiona's hand and held it too close to her face to really see herself.

'You can't show me anything new. I used to see this every morning when I got up, but I don't look any more.'

Fiona held back the hug she wanted to give this girl—a hug to repair some of the damage done to her. Instead she twisted her chair around and sat beside Sophie. With her forefinger she pointed to the big blue eyes glaring back at her from the mirror.

'Not many people's eyes are so dark, almost navy in colour. Very attractive.'

Sophie blinked, stared at herself for a moment before looking away.

'Your hair is shiny and healthy, and, I presume, naturally blonde. The matching eyebrows are a giveaway. And when you smile your whole face lights up. Did you know that?'

After a slight shake of her head the gap between Sophie's face and the mirror increased fractionally. Fiona waited patiently as Sophie ran her tongue around her lips, attempted a small smile, and tried to watch her eyes.

With great care Fiona turned Sophie's face so that they were looking at her right cheek. Then with a gentle movement she eased Sophie around to look at the left side of her face.

'I can't take the scar away, but I can make it a whole lot better. It's unfortunate that the scar runs across the muscles rather than up and down. It will always show a little, and more so when you're tired. I'm going to make the scar less obvious, and over the years it will fade a lot. With the help of make-up you'll be able to hide it—if you want to.'

'I don't believe you.'

'I'm sure you don't, but I'd like you to trust me to help you.' She was asking a lot from a traumatised teen. Whoever had first operated on her injury had not done the best possible job, and now Sophie believed the result to be as good as it would ever get. 'I *can* help, big-time.'

Sophie's enormous eyes were glued to her,

sizing her up, and she felt a jolt of shock as she realised this girl was mature beyond her years.

'That's why I'm here,' Sophie acknowledged.

'Good.' Now Fiona couldn't help herself. She hugged Sophie. 'I'll see you again in the morning. And if you have any questions at all, any time between now and then, even in the middle of the night, get your nurse to call me. She'll know where to find me.'

'Do I have to eat at the hospital?' Sophie's eyes were filled with a mischievous glint.

Not knowing this hospital's protocol, Fiona looked to Tom for guidance.

'As long as you have nothing to eat after eight o'clock tonight you can have whatever you like.' Tom smiled at the girl. 'But if you're thinking of a fast food chain, forget it. The population here is hardly enough to support one of those outlets.'

'Thank goodness for that,' Jacob muttered as he stood up. 'Show me a steak house and I'll be happy.'

'Dad! Not steak again.' Sophie turned imploring eyes onto Tom. 'There are takeaway places here? Aren't there?'

Tom appeared to think about it, until Sophie stared him down.

'There are a few.' He pushed his sleeve back to look at his watch. 'But of course, this is Hanmer Springs. They might've already closed for the night.'

'Dr Tom, you're *so* not fair.'

Fiona listened to the banter while watching Tom. He was at ease with Sophie, gently teasing her, diverting her mind from her operation. He would have been a great father. He *had* been a great father, who'd never got to see his son growing up. For both of them Liam was still five months old, as though stuck in a perpetual state of nappies and breast milk. Other children grew taller, learned to walk and talk, but not Liam. He'd never go to school, ride a bike, kiss a girl. Cot death had stolen him away, along with her heart. Along with Tom's heart.

Her breathing grew tight. Her palms moistened. How she missed her darling boy. How she missed her marriage.

Had Tom ever thought about having another family? Her blood slowed. Why wouldn't he? Then again, he had surrounded himself with a continuous stream of children. Were they his family now? That would be a shame. Tom was definite father material.

She bit down on her lip in an effort to distract herself from the ache that thought brought on. A long time ago she'd made up her mind never to take the risk of having more children. The thought of losing another child almost paralysed her, so nothing would ever change that decision. But she'd hoped Tom might have recovered enough to try again.

Tom returned from showing the Clarks out and made himself comfortable in a chair by propping his legs on the desk. He couldn't get his head around the fact that after all this time Fiona was here, sitting opposite him in his office. It felt bizarre to be talking to her about patients, as though they hadn't had all those years apart. He only had to reach across the desk and he'd be touching her.

Did he want to touch her? So far, every time he had, heated awareness of her had triggered a longing so deep it terrified him. Which meant the coming week would be an ordeal, because she was definitely forbidden territory.

So get back to being professional. Concentrate on why Fiona had come here. Think about the patients whose lives she would be making so much happier. 'You did well with Sophie. It took me three visits to get that far with her. She's had a difficult time coping.'

Fiona's patience with the unhappy teen had surprised him. He had the feeling that she'd have sat with Sophie all night if necessary. But it hadn't been necessary because of her empathy with the girl. Fiona seemed to intrinsically understand where Sophie was coming from, and what she needed from her plastic surgeon.

Patience had *never* been a part of Fiona's make-up. Certainly not with him over the months following Liam's death. She'd got so frustrated when he wouldn't talk about it. At the time he'd been struggling to function enough to get out of bed every morning. In hindsight he could see that neither of them had known how to deal with what had happened. Neither of them had known how to give each other the compassion they'd needed to heal. They'd been too busy using it up on themselves.

Obviously time and events had taught her to stop and listen to people. Earlier he'd been wondering how she'd coped after they separated. He still didn't know the answer to that, but from what he'd seen so far the result was impressive.

Looking at her, he was startled to see a warm glow colouring her cheeks as she replied, 'Thank you. I see a lot of patients despairing because they think no one will want to look at them again. They mainly need listening to.'

How true. 'Teenagers suffer especially. They're so vulnerable when they perceive themselves to be different to their peers.'

'Often their families and friends don't know how to cope with the situation, which adds to their problems.'

Much as they'd both felt when they'd lost Liam, he realised. And *they'd* been adults. Both had been taken up with their own grief, unable to reach out to each other or anyone else. But he should have done more. 'Especially those who try to help.'

A flicker of understanding sparked across Fiona's face. 'We didn't manage very well, did we?'

His jaw clenched. 'There wasn't a manual.' How did anyone know what to do? 'I tried my best for both of us.'

'We both did,' she whispered. The colour drained from her cheeks. Pain flicked into her eyes.

The urge to hold her tight against him, to take that hurt away, swamped him. He longed to stroke her hair, craved her breath against his neck. He wanted to make her feel better. He focused instead on studying her, and was shocked to realise that the inherent sparkle in her eyes had flickered out, gone, replaced by a soul-deep tiredness. His chest tightened as he thought of all the pain she'd endured because of Liam's death and the toll it had taken on her exuberant outlook on life. He looked closer at her drawn face. Was she unwell? Was she up to the job? Of course she was. She wouldn't be here otherwise. That much he trusted.

Gravel crunching under tyres outside reminded him of the trip to the hot pools. 'The haemophiliac patients and their families are waiting on the bus at the front door. They're going to the thermal pools. We always send staff with them, and I like to tag along occasionally. It's fun playing with the kids.'

'I'll see you later, then.' Fiona shuffled files together, her face wistful.

'Come with us. That way you'll get really warm for the first time today.' Now, why the hell had he suggested that when he needed to put space between them?

She shrugged. 'I didn't bring a swimsuit.'

There—problem solved. She wouldn't be joining them at the pool. But the devil had hold of his tongue. 'That's easily fixed. There's a shop next to the pools dedicated to swimming costumes.' Fiona in a swimsuit? His gut clenched.

'It's very tempting.'

'Then grab your purse, and a towel from my bathroom, and meet me at the front steps in five minutes.' He watched her unfurl from the chair and leave his office. He squashed a spurt of fear. In no time at all she'd got under his skin, made him very aware of her. His banging heart seemed more than happy with her arrival. His head said the hospital needed her and that she was proving to be very good with her patients. Exactly what he wanted, demanded, from the specialists who came to work here.

But personally? What did he want? Friendship? Huh! Love? No way. The hell of it was that he didn't have a clue.

Stick to keeping everything on a professional level, remember? Why did he feel he was already off track with that idea? Because now he worried that he'd find himself slipping back into the old habits of their previous life together. Like reaching out to touch her in quiet moments, or making eye contact to pass silent messages in crowded rooms.

Please, no. That would be like starting over, reliving those bleak days when they'd no longer been close enough to be like that. Fiona had left him without a word all those years ago. No warning, no chance to try talking her out of going. She'd just up and gone, leaving him stunned and hurt. He'd believed she'd eventually return, but she hadn't. Not even to explain why she'd had to go.

His heart stuttered. He couldn't lay all the blame on Fiona. The heavy guilt he'd managed to squash into a tiny ball deep inside now churned in his belly, threatening to break out. This time he might have to deal with it.

As the soft warmth of the tepid water seeped into Fiona's chilled muscles she appeared relaxed for the first time since Tom had met her at the airstrip. Even the taut lines around her mouth had receded.

'Coming along with us wasn't such a bad idea,

was it?' He sat down on the edge of the pool beside her. Too close, but it would look silly if he moved now.

'At least I've stopped shivering.' She looked up at him, a hint of warmth in the depths of her beautiful blue eyes.

Funny how he'd never imagined Fiona in this setting with him, and yet now she was here she seemed to fit right in, as though she belonged. Goosebumps rose on his arms. Careful. That was his heart talking. He couldn't trust those emotions when just seeing her still made him feel as though he'd been run over by a truck.

He swung around to scan the pool, found the children from the hospital at the other end clustered around Evan, one of the interns, who was organising them into teams.

'What game can these kids play, considering they've got haemophilia?' Fiona asked beside him.

'There's the problem. Contact sports are out, but how to stop them? We try to organise a version of volleyball, where each player has to stay within their designated space. See those squares painted on the bottom of the pool? The local council did that for us. But it's hard to keep the children in their allocated square. Their parents tell me I worry too much.'

'Guess they're used to having to cope with any resultant bumps.' Fiona watched one of the boys diving under the water to drag a friend beneath the surface.

'Looks like they're about to play bull rush. At least racing each other through the water should be safe from bumps and bangs.'

'Let's join them and have some fun.' Fiona slid into the water, her tee shirt billowing momentarily before absorbing the water and sinking close to her skin, hugging her curves.

His mouth dried. What was it about this woman that always affected him so easily? It seemed that some things never changed.

Someone yelled, 'Come on, Dr Tom! Bet you can't beat me to the end!'

A simple race should be safe. 'An ice cream says I can!'

Hauling himself back onto the side of the pool after the race, Tom sat dangling his feet in the water. He could watch over everyone from here. But it was Fiona that his eyes kept returning to. Time and tragedy had not dimmed her beauty. Her small frame might be slighter than he remembered, but her muscles were still toned and her arms tanned deep walnut. Her dark blonde hair had faded to almost white, no doubt from the sun.

She had said something about wanting to talk to him. Caution snagged his gut. He didn't do talking. But, watching her laughing with young Jordan, he began to wonder if he'd be missing out on something important if he didn't try.

'That surgeon of yours is good with the kids.' One of the fathers sat down beside him. 'See her playing like that and it's hard to imagine she's a plastic surgeon. Maybe she had a thing for embroidery as a kid.'

'Fiona? Needlework?' Tom spluttered. 'Don't be fooled by her appearance. When Fiona wants to have fun you'll find her white water rafting, parachuting, or flying a plane. You will never find her embroidering.'

But then a memory teased the edge of his mind, grew vivid. Fiona bent over an aged cream-coloured robe, carefully repairing a small tear in the generations-old family garment. She'd done it for Liam to wear at his christening. The christening they'd never had. Pain slid in under his skin, wrapped around his heart. His son had died too soon. Years too soon. No parent should outlive their child.

A cry from across the pool snapped through his mind. He jerked his head up, searched the pool. In the middle, Fiona pushed through the water towards two lads, Morgan and Baden. With his heart in his throat, Tom dropped into the pool and swam to join them.

'What happened?' he demanded.

'It's okay, I just banged my arm on Morgan's head,' Baden tried to reassure Tom.

But he wasn't taking the boy's word that everything was all right. 'Get out of the water so I can take a look. You too, Morgan. Out,' Tom ordered. This was exactly what he'd been afraid of.

Fiona hoisted herself out of the water and turned to give Baden a hand. With the boys out, and Fiona checking Baden, Tom concentrated on Morgan. For the second time that day they were working together, and it felt good.

Evan brought across the medical bag that went on every outing. It contained, amongst the usual medical requirements, a supply of clotting factors and vitamin K to cover such events as this.

'Do we know which factor Baden needs?' Fiona asked.

'Type A,' Baden told her.

'There are notes in the bag.' Tom fingered Morgan's head, then reached into the bag for vials of Vitamin K, handed one to Fiona.

Baden didn't seem at all perturbed by the sudden turn of events. 'I'm used to it,' he said in reply to Fiona's query about how he felt. 'It was an accident anyway.'

'Let me check you out first, okay?' Her fingers were moving carefully over his arm. Within minutes both boys were back on their feet, laughing and teasing each other over who had the biggest bruise as they headed to the changing room.

Tom tried to relax. But inside he was winding up tighter and tighter. The boys were so unconcerned about the whole thing. Didn't they understand the seriousness of any little knock?

Fiona spoke quietly beside him. 'Baden's right. It was an accident.'

'It still shouldn't have happened.'

Her fingers brushed his hand at his side. 'Their parents probably spend a lot of time trying to create a normal life for them, while at the same time worrying themselves sick about accidents.

The kids have come here for a wonderful experience and that's what they're having.' Her hand gently squeezed his as she continued. 'You've done that for them. By the nature of their condition there's already plenty of discipline in their lives. With what you're doing here you're giving them confidence to try other things. You mustn't take it away in the same breath.'

His hand closed around her fingers. The tension ebbed as her words sank in. Because she was right. Sometimes he worried too much. He gulped. He was their paediatrician, not their parent. Out of the blue Fiona had done that for him. The ground tilted beneath his feet, and he felt afraid. If she had the power to put him back on track so easily then what else could she do to him?

'I'm going to change. That water might be warm but the air's chilly.' She tugged her hand away and turned to the women's changing rooms before he could thank her.

He watched her avoiding skidding on the wet concrete, tugging her sopping wet tee shirt over her head as she went. Beneath the shirt she wore a bikini the shade of her eyes. His favourite colour on her. Had she remembered that? Unlikely. From behind she looked lovely, her skin translucent in the eerie overhead lighting. Her wet hair clung to her slender neck. His gaze followed her until she'd gone, lost amongst the chattering young girls charging inside out of the cold air to change.

Startled at his thoughts, Tom growled and went to change too. The rough chatter and laughter of the boys didn't drown out the pictures crashing around in his skull. All pictures of Fiona. Of course she was different from how he remembered. Who wouldn't be after what they'd been through? Also, six years was a long time. He saw a softness about her now that hadn't been there before.

Face it, he couldn't believe she'd changed that much. He didn't trust that she might have. Once she'd proved how untrustworthy she could be, and once was enough.

CHAPTER FOUR

Tom sat in the front seat of the bus and watched Fiona laughing and chatting with one of the mums as they came out of the pool complex. He tingled at the mere sight of her. A breath of fresh air in his harried world. She brought reminders of other things with her—things he hadn't devoted much attention to in a long time. Family. Marriage. Plain old fun, for heaven's sake. Occasionally he did a spot of trout fishing with Pierce, the local cop, but that was as fun as his private life got these days.

Fiona's head popped through the bus door, her eyes searching for a seat. The one beside him beckoned. The woman behind her gave Fiona a nudge towards it, and slipped past to another spare seat.

Tom tapped his watch. 'We've got a busload of starving kids here. You two want to explain to them why we're waiting?'

Fiona rolled her eyes at him. 'Women's stuff. You'd never in a million years understand.'

'Damn right. My feminine side is very undernourished. I intend keeping it that way, too.'

'Phew. For a moment there you had me worried.' Amusement filled her eyes as her bottom wriggled into the cramped space beside him, her hip bumping his, her thigh touching his thigh.

His mouth dried. There was absolutely nothing wrong with his masculine side. It knew her body inside out. It wanted her body. On a bus full of shouting kids? Well, there had been a drought. Even on the rare times he had dated his response to those women hadn't been as urgent as this. Fiona was one very sexy lady, even when she'd turned up after so long, shocking him to Hades and back.

The bus lurched forward, catching Fiona unawares, and she grabbed at his leg. Where her fingers dug in heat flared, expanded up and down his already wired body. How fickle were his hormones? He had to get control back. *One, two, three, four...*

'At least my bones are warmer after that swim.' Fiona whipped her hand away and turned to face him, creating a gap between them.

'Bones don't get cold.' Was that a responding tension lurking in the corners of her eyes?

She rolled those eyes again. 'As of today, mine do.'

'Then I guess you won't want to go skiing while you're here.'

Caution tripped across her face. 'Is that an invitation? I didn't think I'd have time for anything much more than work.'

Was he inviting her to spend time with him? He tilted back against the side of the bus to avoid her intent gaze and thought quickly. Would he like to take her up the mountain for a ski? She didn't know this region and it would be fun to show her around. Hang on. Wasn't he supposed to be keeping this relationship strictly professional? 'You're right. There won't be enough free hours for outdoor activities.'

Her shoulders drooped. In her lap, her fingers fiddled with the corner of her damp towel. So he'd let her down, and now he felt a heel, but better not to get too involved with her outside of the hospital.

Changing the subject, he asked, 'Are you still a bit of a daredevil?'

The fingers stopped their fidgeting. 'If you're

asking do I still take on the world at every opportunity, just to prove to my father that I'm as good as my brother would've been if he'd lived into adulthood, then no. When I fly these days it's with caution. When I'm behind the steering wheel of a car I'm slower than an eighty-year-old.'

She'd made him angry with her recklessness. 'I'm glad to hear you've quietened down. You used to worry the hell out of me.'

'Do you have any good memories of me? Of our time together?'

Shock cracked him over the head. 'Of course I do.' If only she knew. There were so many he couldn't count them. *She would know just how many memories you hold if you told her.* His skin prickled. Tell Fiona about those? That would mean getting close and personal, and he was not prepared to do that. That would let her creep back in under his skin, and then he might have to start all over again exorcising her from his heart. He doubted he had the strength to go through that a second time.

She muttered, 'If you give me a chance I think you'll find that I tend to put other people first these days.'

'I never thought you were selfish. For a start you're a doctor, and by the very nature of doctors you can't be. Doctors help people by giving—their skills, their time, their compassion.' But she had been on a mission to prove how clever she was all the time, which had been hard to live with.

Her eyes widened and a tentative smile grew, sending warmth through his starved soul. He'd missed that smile. It was the first thing he'd looked for on waking every morning, and in the weeks after she'd left his heart had broken all over again every time he'd rolled over in bed to find his day wasn't about to start with a sunny smile.

'Thank you,' she whispered. 'I didn't know you thought that.'

Surely he'd told her? What a mess they'd made of everything.

'Didn't we?' she agreed.

That was when he realised he'd spoken aloud.

She added, 'We really bungled everything. If only we'd known how to talk to each other.'

'Neither of us was at fault for not saving our marriage. We were out of our depth back then.' Damn it, he was out of his depth *now*. Talking had never been his strong point. Actions were stronger, more eloquent, than anything he could verbalise. There would be no actions with Fiona, though. Not now, and not at any time during the coming week.

Fiona leaned against Tom's kitchen door, shaking her head at the small table he'd set ready for dinner. A chuckle pushed up her throat.

Tom spun around from the vegetables he was preparing, his eyebrows lifted. 'What?'

'You still do that.' She nodded at the cutlery placed very straight beside the placemats, at the glasses square to the top right corner of the mats. Carefully folded serviettes were under each fork. She waved her hand at the table. 'Line everything up perfectly.' She slipped across the room and moved the forks so that they were at angles to the placemats. Then she shifted the glasses. And gave Tom a satisfied smirk.

'And *you* always did that,' he said.

'And then you always straightened them up again.'

'It's a sign of an orderly mind.'

'Not that old excuse,' she laughed.

'It's the only one I've got.'

Sometimes she'd used to mess up his settings and then stand with her back to the table, as though defending her changes. And sometimes she'd demand a kiss before letting him at the table, and that had inevitably led to the bedroom.

Her smile faltered. She didn't need to remember that right now. Glancing at him she found him staring at her, his mouth open in an O. She saw recognition of those same memories in his eyes.

After a long moment she crossed to the stove to see what Tom was cooking. When she thought her voice would sound normal she commented, with as much nonchalance she could muster, 'I haven't had a decent steak in ages.'

'Still like it medium rare?'

She thought she heard a hitch in his voice. Standing close to him, she smelt a faint whiff of that morning's aftershave, overlaid with chlorine from the pool. It distracted her, brought her focus to his hands as they deftly sliced broccoli florets. Confident hands that could evoke all sorts of heated responses from her body. She swallowed hard.

'Well-done these days,' she croaked. 'We couldn't always trust the meat where we worked, so cooking it very thoroughly became our safety measure.' She opened the fridge to rummage around, adding, 'Actually, I *will* try medium rare.'

'You might find you can't take the taste now.'

She made the mistake of looking at him. *Taste.* What she wanted to taste was his tantalising mouth. What she really wanted was to kiss him!

No, she didn't. She couldn't.

She did. She could.

'Fiona? Your steak?'

She wouldn't. Her steak? Oh, yes, that's right. 'I'll give the medium rare a go. I can always put it back in the pan if I don't like it.' In the fridge she found the juice. 'What do you want to drink?'

'There's a bottle of red in the pot cupboard.'

'Pot cupboard? Who are you hiding it from? The cleaning lady?' She tugged open the door he indicated beside the stove, staying well clear of his legs. Of him. She didn't breathe in case his aftershave distracted her again.

'I don't have a lot of cupboard space in here.' Tom moved a step further away. Keeping his distance too?

When Fiona had poured his glass of Pinot she

placed it on the bench, carefully avoiding any inadvertent touch of his hand. She had to keep her imagination under control and remember why she was here. 'There you go.'

'Thanks. You don't want wine instead of juice?'

'I'm not a red wine fan—never have been.'

So far it seemed to be the only thing he had forgotten. She imagined there were plenty of things he wished he couldn't recall.

They ate in silence. Fiona devoured her steak and the sautéed vegetables as though she hadn't eaten for days.

'It's been a long time since breakfast,' she said as she pushed her plate aside and picked up her juice. 'That was great, thank you. You cook a mean steak.'

'All compliments accepted.'

'Tasty vegetables, too. I've missed fresh green vegetables.' She picked up her fork and speared a courgette stick from his plate.

'Don't mind me.' He watched her nibbling at the vegetable, his throat working overtime.

This kitchen felt small, claustrophobic. Tom's presence filled the spaces and heated the air. It stole her determination to ignore everything except her role as a surgeon, for tonight at least, so that Tom had time to get used to her being around.

His chair screeched over the tiles when he shoved back. Picking up their empty plates, he placed them neatly in the sink before topping up his wine glass.

As she watched him Fiona stretched back, pushed her legs out under the table. 'Why did you decide to open a small children's hospital? Couldn't you have done the same thing within the public sector?'

Tom straddled his chair, resting his arms across the back, his glass in one hand. 'I wasn't getting the level of satisfaction I felt I should. No matter how many children I saw, there were countless others waiting. I was driven to help more and more.'

'Because of Liam? This is your way of dealing with what happened?' Understanding tugged at her.

His head dipped in acknowledgment. 'Probably. Yes.'

'We both seem to have immersed ourselves in work to forget the past.'

'Not to forget. To accept, and maybe to move on,' he corrected her.

'You're right. I'll never forget.' She paused, wishing she did enjoy red wine, because right now she could do with a hefty slug of something stronger than juice. Just to take the edge off the pain of remembering her baby. Being with Tom brought Liam so close she felt she only had to reach out and she'd be able to touch him. *Don't do this. He's not here. But Tom is, and you need to concentrate on finding a way through to him.* Her teeth dug into her bottom lip as she waited for the pain to pass.

Tom seemed unaware of her agitation. 'Work is supposed to be a panacea for grief.' He shrugged. 'Who knows? I did what I thought was right at the time.'

'Avoiding talking about Liam didn't seem right to me.' The words spilled over her lips before she thought about them.

Tom's face darkened. The fingers holding the wine glass tightened, putting the narrow stem at risk. 'I thought we'd agreed we didn't have a manual on grief.'

The shutters came down over his eyes.

She searched her mind for a safer subject and

returned to their previous topic. 'Where did the idea for a paediatric hospital come from? I never guessed you wanted something like this.'

The glass turned slowly in fingers that were beginning to relax. 'The system used by hospital boards across the country for seeing patients is, of necessity, slow and tedious. Appointments are made months away, and then a high percentage of people don't keep them, which makes for wasted time and lots of sick people going without treatment for far too long.'

'But surely you have just as many patients not making their appointments here?'

'Very few, in fact. Possibly because our approach is more personal. I've tried to make the system more user-friendly, accommodating everyone's needs. I'm talking costs, transport, having family staying while a child is in hospital.' He sipped his wine.

'I'd have thought the one thing wrong with being in Hanmer Springs is the distance from big cities and the greater population base.'

'The other way round, in fact. Everyone loves coming here. All the outdoor activities are an added attraction, which some families take advantage of during or after their stay with us.

The hot pools are always popular, too. As for initial consultations, I go to Christchurch and Dunedin, taking specialists with me if necessary, and for those that can't afford to travel here Social Welfare helps out.'

'Funding must be a constant battle.' Fiona flicked her finger and thumb. 'I wish I'd known earlier. I could've helped in that respect.'

'Thank you, but that's the main reason you never knew about this idea. You would've wanted to coerce your father into backing me financially, and I'd have had to fight you all the way. It was my dream, and I wanted to keep that alive, not have to argue with you all the way.'

She opened her mouth to protest, but he was right. She would have tried to take over. That was how she'd done things back then.

'Anyway, we weren't ready for such a big project. We'd only been married two years. We had a baby to think about. I was prepared to wait a few years.'

'This was your big dream, your life's ambition, and you didn't share it. I do understand why, but—' She shook her head at him. She couldn't ignore the hurt that he hadn't told her.

The look in her eyes must have unsettled him. He rose from his chair and lifted the wine glass to his mouth, drained it. 'Look, Fiona, I've got to go across to the office. There are some urgent letters waiting for me to sign. Not to mention a stack of paperwork.'

He was getting away from her. No doubt he thought she was about to get stuck into him about not showing any faith in her. What he didn't know was that despite her hurt she agreed with him. He'd done the right thing for himself.

He said in a conciliatory tone, 'I'll see you in the morning. Eight o'clock start.'

She nodded. 'That's what this place is all about—looking out for as many children as possible.'

'That and trying to prevent as many parents as possible having to deal with the agony and anguish you and I suffered when we lost Liam.'

When the front door had closed behind Tom she sat, staring blankly at the wall of photos. *That went well, Fiona. You really wound the man up. Why did you have to attack him? Now he'll avoid you as much as possible. A fat lot of good that'll do to your chances of righting the wrongs of the past. And now you're on your own for the rest of the evening. There have been too many long, lonely nights for you to welcome another one.*

* * *

Fiona stepped back from the operating table the next day and placed her hands on the small of her back, arching backwards to relieve the dull ache that had set in an hour ago. She'd done four operations since daybreak. 'What an amazing set-up you've got here. I haven't worked in such a modern operating theatre for years, if ever.'

'Not bad, is it?' Tom looked around the room with pride, as though seeing it for the first time.

She liked that he could still get a buzz out of it. 'Not bad? You don't know you're alive. The best bit is the lack of flies.'

'Flies? You are joking!' Kerry exclaimed as she stood up from her equipment, stretching her arms.

'Unfortunately not.' She shuddered. 'I never got used to them.'

'Who were you working for abroad?' Kerry asked.

'While I finished qualifying in London I kept hearing about Global Health. GH is dedicated to taking specialist healthcare to countries where many less fortunate people would otherwise never get the help they need. There were some glowing reports about the work their teams were doing, and those eventually made me feel working for GH would be right for me.'

She'd felt restless and unmotivated about her future. Initially Global Health had been an opportunity to move around without tying herself into a long-term contract.

She continued, 'They sent me to Romania, Indonesia, and lastly to Pakistan.'

'I admit to being a little surprised when I read that in your CV.' Tom's wide-eyed stare made her want to chuckle. 'You really did reinvent yourself.'

'Just a tad.' A wry smile twisted her mouth. Tom's comments were nothing new. Many people said the same thing—especially people who'd known her when she'd lived in the lap of luxury in Auckland.

Fiona fully understood. When she'd left Tom she'd had no intention of spending her career in places where hot showers, soft beds and good food were not an option. They were comforts she'd taken for granted. No, she'd been destined to be the best plastic surgeon in private practice.

'You worked in a plastic surgery team?' Kerry asked.

'No, each team consists of six to eight different

specialists. Cardiology is one of the most common specialties catered for, but they can use just about any specialist.' Fiona thought about the doctors in her team. 'Paediatricians are always in demand. The children in poor countries have some horrendous illnesses, and usually they have no option but to tough it out. Or die.' Which many of them did. She'd never got used to that. There were nights she'd lie awake feeling the mothers' agony.

Above his mask, Tom's eyes were thoughtful. 'How did you deal with those deaths?'

'By operating on as many other people as possible. It was never enough.' He'd know what she meant by that. He'd also know none of those children she'd helped had brought Liam back to her.

'What were the hospitals like that you worked in?' Tom asked. 'Pakistan has some good ones, but I don't know much about the other countries you mentioned.'

'You're right, there are some great hospitals in most of the countries I went to, but for the Global Health teams hospitals weren't always an option. Certainly we didn't work in the big modern ones. Often we had the use of a hall or a school, occasionally tents. Power could be erratic. I've had to finish suturing under torchlight but I don't recommend it.'

There had been a lot of wonderful aspects about the job, but now standing here in this ultra-modern theatre, the last three years of her life seemed impossibly remote. As though she'd been working on Mars. And she didn't know at the moment how she felt about going back to Global Health after her leave was up. The thought of not returning at all had slipped into her mind a couple of times. She didn't really know what she wanted to do.

Was she subconsciously moving on from that nomadic lifestyle? Looking to settle in one place? Make a home for herself? Automatically she looked to Tom and found his piercing gaze still fixed on her. A huge question filled those eyes, one she couldn't read. What did he want from her?

She'd forgotten they weren't alone until Kerry interrupted her distracted thoughts with, 'So, the equipment you used would be fairly basic?'

'Absolutely—which is why, while I'm in New Zealand, I intend applying pressure to every hospital board in the country for any so-called obsolete equipment they have lying around forgotten in cupboards and storerooms.'

'Are you going back to your job with this organisation?' Tom asked, his expression remote, his shoulders tense.

'My contract has expired but I can pick up a new one whenever I'm ready. GH has a policy of enforcing staff to take leave at the end of three years if they haven't taken any sooner. It's not a normal way of life, and they find their staff suffer burnout otherwise.' Which didn't give him a yes or a no. How could she tell him something she didn't know yet? Incredibly, a strange sense of belonging had been slowly creeping over her ever since first setting eyes on Tom yesterday. Like a missing piece falling back into place.

She'd loved wandering from country to country, village to village, but at this very minute, in this hospital, doubts were bombarding her. Seeing the haven Tom had created for himself within his hospital seemed to be cultivating a deep need within her for roots, a place to call her own.

Unfortunately a divorce would be the logical next step. Odd that neither of them had ever instigated one. Goosebumps lifted her skin. Did she want one now? Deep down, she didn't think so. Did Tom want one?

Thankfully Kerry again interrupted her thoughts. 'I don't know about the rest of you, but I'm going to lunch.'

Fiona decided to go later. 'I'm going to pop up and see Sophie first. She should be wide awake by now.'

Tom tossed his latex gloves into a hazardous substance bin. 'I'll come with you.'

Fiona frowned. She'd have preferred to go alone, to take a break from Tom's questioning scrutiny. 'I'm sure Sophie and her father will be glad to see you.'

Tom shrugged. 'Look, this is how I do things around here. These are my patients.'

'Fair enough.' She'd presumed he'd leave alone the specialists he brought in, only helping where needed. But this way he had first-hand knowledge of everything being done. She had to admit she liked that.

His hand wrapped around her wrist and tugged at her gently, until she jerked her head up to meet his level gaze. 'I'm glad you understand.'

His fingers warmed her, sending unexpected shockwaves throughout her body, reminding her how his touch had so easily turned her on. But memories were dangerous territory. They could do untold damage to her heart, and create havoc with her hard-earned peace of mind.

'Sure.' She pulled her arm away, rubbing where he'd touched. 'How long have we got before our next patient?'

Tom had assisted in Theatre all morning. He'd been very professional and competent. No surprise there. Tom was a highly skilled doctor. But to Fiona his greatest asset had to be his interest in his patients and his willingness to listen to them. Odd how he could listen to a patient describing their ailments but he hadn't been able to hear his own wife when she'd wanted to talk to him.

He said, 'Nearly an hour's break. Maybe we should grab a bite of lunch first, then go check up on your post-op patients.'

Her stomach rumbled at the mention of food. Last night's dinner seemed an age ago, and she'd had nothing for breakfast this morning as she'd been too nervous about working with Tom. No wonder she was ravenous. 'Hope someone killed a horse for lunch.'

'Don't mention eating horse meat around here.

You'll be run out of town, exceptional plastic surgeon or not.' Tom smiled at her.

Exceptional, huh? Warmth flooded her, lightened her step. Another compliment that she'd treasure. 'Okay, I'll settle for a loaf of bread and a hunk of ham.'

'I hope the kitchen staff can cope while you're here. I haven't forgotten your phenomenal appetite.'

'For what?' she blurted, and instantly coloured. Sex had come to her mind straight away.

'Food.' Tom scowled, but in his eyes she saw him register her meaning. His stride lengthened, and once again she had to trot to keep up.

'Right, food,' she muttered. *Not sex.* The one area of their relationship they'd never had trouble with. Her thumb flicked her fingers. Her mind had developed an unnerving habit of throwing her off balance. Think sandwich, not hot skin. Think ham, not slick tongues.

Don't think at all.

After a quick lunch with Tom and Kerry, Fiona headed for Sophie's room. With Tom beside her, of course.

'Sophie's awake and asking questions of any

medical staff looking in on her,' the girl's nurse informed them.

'Hey, young lady, how're you doing?' Fiona asked as she approached the bed.

Sophie was pale, and there were dark shadows under her apprehensive eyes, but she was awake enough to be aware of everything going on around her. 'How did it go? Am I going to look better than I did before?'

'You were a perfect patient, sleeping right through everything.' Fiona sat down on the edge of the bed and winked. 'Seriously, I'm very pleased with the operation. I did warn you that your scar will look worse before it heals. Be patient, if you can. You're going to look fantastic. Remember, you're a beautiful girl.'

Seated on the other side of the bed, Jacob Clark smiled wearily. 'You're asking a teenager to be patient? You can't have any children of your own.'

She closed her eyes as her stomach curled around the permanent knot of pain. Just because Liam wasn't here now it didn't mean she wasn't a mother. But it was easier to go along with Jacob's assumption. 'No, I haven't.'

When she opened her eyes she found Tom's

gaze on her, deep sadness etched in the lines of his face. His eyes were dark, the caution that had mostly been there since she arrived replaced with sorrow. In the depths of his eyes she found a mirror image of her pain. She still wondered how he managed, surrounded by children every day. Surely that ate away at him sometimes?

Shame gripped her. By coming here she'd made everything that much harder for Tom to live with. He probably managed relatively well, but her arrival would have dragged up as much hurt for him as it had for her.

She hoped she'd survive the onslaught of emotions that had been battering her since her arrival.

Tom made an instant decision. He mightn't be great shakes at talking about personal things, but he could certainly show Fiona what he'd achieved since they'd broken up, and she'd be able to see what it all meant to him. 'Come on, we've got plenty of time before surgery. I'll give you the grand tour of my hospital.'

'I'd love that. Everything I've seen so far is amazing.'

Warmth unfurled in his belly at her simple but

genuine words. 'I'm afraid the rest of the building hasn't been modernised like the operating theatre.'

Of course his earlier intention of keeping his distance from Fiona had gone down the drain. For some reason it wasn't as easy to stick to as he'd believed. After her dig last night about him always working he'd thought he might have been cured of whatever was drawing him closer to her. He'd been wrong. All morning he hadn't been able to keep his eyes off her as she operated. Watching her perform intricate surgery had been a revelation. No doubt about it. Fiona's skill level was impressive. He'd enjoyed assisting her. His patients were lucky to have her.

And he was beginning to understand how she'd coped over the years since she'd left. She must have focused entirely on her surgical work, continuously expanding her knowledge and practical skills while pushing aside the hurt and anger at what had happened to them. Being around people who desperately needed her, being able to give them not just good care but superb care, would have been good for her soul.

She was speaking.

'New paint and equipment go a long way

towards instilling confidence in your patients. But really they come here for your expertise as a paediatrician.'

'You're right, of course.' As Tom held a door open for Fiona her perfume scented the air around him, teasing him and causing him to stop to take a good long look at her. Her once bouncy step was now more measured, the jaunty angle of her head not so apparent, but the woman before him was still the Fi he remembered. Her enquiring eyes took in everything around her; her quick mind noted all the little things about her patients that were so important to a full and quick recovery.

'Tom?' Fiona had turned back, those blue eyes asking *why the delay?*

'Coming. Reception is through here.' They were on the ground floor, where the operating theatre and staffrooms were. 'Then in the west wing we have the consultation rooms. Except for mine. I like having a view, which is why my offices are on the next floor.'

'Boss's privilege.' Fiona gazed around the reception area that had been positioned around the main entrance and a sweeping staircase. 'Those are gorgeous.' She pointed to the stained-glass front doors.

The second floor held the wards. 'Two: one for the boys and one for the girls, with the nurses' station between them.'

Tom tried to stifle a yawn and failed. Thankfully Fiona's attention was taken up with looking around, so she didn't notice.

A sleepless night hadn't helped his unsettled mood. Staying up until after midnight working on the next six months of patient figures hadn't tired him as much as he'd hoped.

'We'll carry on to the top floor first. You can take a good look around the wards on the way down if you want to.'

'Of course I want to. Tom.' She spun around to face him, walking backwards as she waved her hands in the air, talking fast. 'This is astonishing. You've achieved so much here in a relatively short time. You must be so proud.'

'I am a bit.'

'A bit?' Her eyes widened and her mouth split into a wide grin. She shrugged her shoulders and deepened her voice. 'He's a little bit proud. That's all.'

He laughed. As he was meant to. 'Come on. Top floor is waiting.'

She raced up the stairs, looking from behind

like a child, not a surgeon with a serious workload ahead of her. He followed more slowly. Last night when he'd been trying to sleep Fiona had filled his head to the point where he'd thought he'd go crazy. Her sharp words about them making a mess of everything back then had crashed around in his skull, haunting him with her pain. What she didn't understand was that he'd tried to do everything right for them both. He'd taken care of all the funeral arrangements to save her that agony. When she hadn't had the energy to get out of bed he'd taken over the mundane chores around the house that she'd usually seen to. He'd watched out for her at the hospital when she'd returned to work and arranged that any very young patients were seen by another plastic surgeon. When she'd cried for hours on end he'd held her close. He'd listened to every word she'd said—day and night, even when he'd been so exhausted he couldn't concentrate. He'd really, really tried. It hadn't been enough.

But it wasn't only his sleep she'd interrupted last night. She'd already permeated the hospital: popping up everywhere, chatting with the nurses, reassuring her patients. Even when she wasn't present she might as well have been, the way the staff talked about her. He grunted. Talking about her relationship with him, most likely. Already he found himself straining to hear her laughter at unexpected moments.

'So, the third floor. What goes on here?' Fiona brought his attention back to the here and now.

He quickly showed her around. There wasn't a lot to see, as this floor hadn't been fully developed yet. 'I haven't got a need for it so far, but the time will come when I do require more space.'

At the top of the stairs, ready to head back down, Fiona threw a wild card at him.

'Tom, where did we go wrong? Why couldn't we communicate back then?'

And he'd thought she couldn't shock him any more. 'Because we were grief stricken. Because our marriage was running on empty.'

'When I look around and see what you've achieved in a relatively short time I know you must have had to negotiate, wheedle, cajole, and occasionally demand all sorts of support from people. Then I think of the things I've done, the people I've worked with and for, and I can't help but wonder why we couldn't have applied those skills to sorting out our marriage.' She leaned against the balustrade and crossed her ankles.

He stared at her, looking for trouble in her demeanour, finding only open frankness. She really wanted an answer. If only he had one.

'I don't know. I've spent untold hours thinking through those weeks before you left. I've tried to see what I could've done differently and I've never come up with an answer.' Except to do as she'd demanded. But at the time words just wouldn't have made the slightest bit of difference to all the pain and anger he'd been feeling. 'I admit to being afraid that if I started talking then the rage I felt at the unfairness of what had happened would burst out and I'd never get control back.'

She nodded slowly, understanding filtering through her eyes. 'I see.'

He waited for the fireworks. When they didn't come, he lifted her hand and squeezed it gently. 'Come on. We've got surgery to perform.'

She followed quietly. Too quietly for his liking. That only gave him more to worry about.

CHAPTER FIVE

AFTERNOON surgery lasted until a little after four. Fiona repaired the harelip on the ten-year-old boy who should have had the surgery when he was a baby and there were two patients for skin grafts.

Fiona went to see young Shaun Elliott and his parents in his room after she'd finished in Theatre.

'How is he?' his father asked. 'I mean, did the operation go well, or will Shaun need more surgery in the future?'

'I'm very confident we've done all we can for him. Unless something goes wrong over the next few weeks Shaun has had his last skin graft. I also tidied up that scar that runs across the back of his hand.'

'By something going wrong, you mean infection, don't you?' Shaun's mother asked, her worry causing a frown. 'He had a problem with that last time and it took for ever to heal. It's so hard to see him putting up with the pain and trying to keep his hand still.'

Fiona nodded. 'Yes, I'm referring to infection, and because of his history I'm giving him a heavy dose of antibiotics right from the start.' Fiona looked down at the tiny figure under the bedcovers. 'He's small for his age. Does he eat well?'

'He's always been a picky eater,' his mother replied. 'It doesn't matter what I put before him, he doesn't get excited about food.'

'Maybe when Shaun's got over this operation you should look into that. I know children can be fussy about food, but he needs to be eating well. The infections he gets might be explained by the fact he's lacking in nutrients and vitamins.'

'I'll give him a check-up while he's here.' A familiar voice cut across the room.

Fiona spun around. She hadn't heard Tom arrive. Her heart thumped at the sight of his tall frame filling the doorway.

'If that's all right with you both?' Tom asked Shaun's parents.

'Absolutely. We've taken Shaun to our family doctor, but she tells us not to worry, that he'll grow out of it in time. But we are worried. He turned seven last month, and at his party I couldn't believe how much all his friends ate compared to him.'

Seven. Fiona looked at the boy, who had the body size of a small five-year-old. His cute face, despite being pale, made her itch to reach out and smooth back the fair curls lying on his forehead. Her heart squeezed. 'Seven years old. It's such an innocent time of life.'

Although not for Shaun. He'd had to deal with the results of an accident for more than a year now. But it wasn't this particular seven-year-old she thought about. Liam would have been turning seven in two months time. Her fists clenched, and then she felt a hand on her shoulder, gentle fingers pressing through her clothes. Turning, she met Tom's intense gaze, saw the understanding there.

Tears pricked her eyelids. A crazy, out-of-place reaction. She hadn't been this bad for a long time. She dropped her head, stared blindly at the floor, striving for control. She didn't need sympathy. Especially not from Tom. It would be her undoing.

With a quick toss of her head, she said vaguely

in the direction of the boy's parents, 'I'll call in again later tonight to check on Shaun.'

Then she left the room and walked rapidly along the ward, determined to get away from Tom for a while. A walk in the grounds would be just the thing. The fresh air would clear her head after a big day in Theatre. Fresh air and time alone.

But, wrapped in the thicker of the two jerseys she'd brought and her jacket, she couldn't stop the images of Tom popping into her mind as she wandered around the expansive hospital grounds. All day he'd acted as her assistant, a highly competent one too, with an uncanny knack of predicting what she needed almost before she did. Then there was the way patients responded to him during ward rounds. He'd lightened up a lot over the intervening years, but his manner still remained firm and definitely more serious than hers.

Huh. She laughed mirthlessly. A clown in a circus would have been more serious than the old her. But not now. These days she didn't find a lot to poke the finger at, nor did she laugh much. And she did not treat her life as cheaply as she once had.

A sigh slid through her chilled lips. One of Tom's pet hates had been her flagrant disregard for rules and regulations, and her continuous need to test herself against the odds.

Tom had definitely been the sensible one in their relationship. The exhilaration of soaring across the sky in a two-seater aeroplane, deliberately stalling the engine to have the thrill of flinging it into a spin before pulling out five hundred feet above the ground had not been for him. But she'd been driven by a continuous need to prove how good she could be.

Tom, Tom, Tom. He filled her head. His scent in the air as he worked opposite her in theatre, his voice echoing in the corridors of the hospital. Damn, but this had become so hard, so fast.

'Hey, lady, who are you?' A young voice penetrated her bleak thoughts.

'I'm Fiona. Who are you?' She studied the muddy urchin before her. He oozed mischief, from his cheeky grin to his small fists balled against skinny hips.

'Connor. My mum does the gardens around the hospital. Dr Tom says she's very good.' His chin jutted out, as though daring her to disagree.

'She must be. The grounds are beautiful. Does she do them all on her own?'

'Not quite. Someone helps her.' The chin lost some of its severity, and the boy shrugged. 'What do you do? Are you another doctor?'

Fiona grinned. 'I'm afraid so. Don't you like doctors?'

He shrugged. 'They're all right. I like Dr Tom cos he gives me jobs and pays me.'

'What sort of jobs?' Seemed like Tom looked out for everyone around here, not just his patients.

'I have to collect the eggs. Do you want to see the hens?'

'I'd love to.' She fell into stride beside her new friend.

Connor rolled his eyes, clearly not impressed with her lack of knowledge. 'They've got places outside where they lay the eggs.'

The gardening sheds were behind the hospital, and beside them stood the chicken coop. Connor led her inside the coop and picked up a gold and brown hen, cuddling her in his arms. 'You can carry the egg basket if you like.'

'Okay. How many eggs are we going to find?'

'Lots and lots.'

Connor chattered non-stop for the next half-hour as he went from the bushes to the hedge to the vegetable garden, gathering up his bounty.

Fiona happily followed him, learning that he was ten, and his sister was four and a pain. School was fun, but his mum taught him better things, like how to grow pumpkins in summer and cauliflowers in winter.

'I have to go now.' Connor carefully took the basket from Fiona. 'I have to clean the shed and take these eggs to the hospital kitchen.'

'Okay. I might see you again during the week.' Fiona watched Connor skip away, ever mindful of his precious load, before she turned and headed in the direction of the cottage. She suddenly felt very alone.

If only she had someone to share what was bothering her. It was Tom she really wanted to talk to, but so far he wasn't very forthcoming. *Back up.* His revelation last night, about how his need to save other parents from what they had been through had driven him to create this specialist hospital, had been more than she'd got in months last time they were together.

Tom mightn't have verbalised his thoughts, but

this place showed how he truly felt. She'd always been the talkative one, he the quieter, steadier one. The rock in their relationship. But rocks cracked. Had she even given him a chance to explain how he was coping without going on at him, demanding he talk to her? Her heart squeezed painfully. She'd always thought she'd tried so hard to comfort him, but maybe she hadn't seen what he'd really wanted.

Everyone dealt with grief differently. But had she considered that at the time they were both dealing with Liam's death? If she could be frank with herself the answer would be no. She hadn't. Instead she'd hounded Tom to be like her, act like her. As if he could have. What had she done to him? Hurt him even more by not giving him space to grieve. No wonder he didn't want her back in his life for even a few days.

When she reached the front door to the cottage and heard the television blaring out the news bulletin, she found she couldn't face Tom with these thoughts tripping around her head, so she turned and headed for the hospital. She'd take another look at today's patients. Tomorrow's would be in the dining hall, having dinner with their families by now, so she'd see them later.

And face Tom later still.

Sophie sat propped up with two pillows when Fiona entered her room.

'Hey, how's things?' Fiona asked.

'Very sore. And I look like I've been dragged behind a car on my face.'

'That's not how I'd have described my handiwork.' Fiona sat on the edge of the bed.

'I'm so swollen I don't seem to have a face any more. Didn't like it anyway, so maybe that's a plus.' Sophie was glum, and definitely feeling sorry for herself.

'You'd prefer no face at all? Then people would really stare at you.'

'They already do.'

Fiona reached for the teen's hands that were scrunching up the pages of the magazine she'd been pretending to read.

'Listen to me. Have you ever considered that people may be looking at you because you're lovely, not because you've got a scar?'

When Sophie said nothing, she continued, 'People will always look at you when they are with you, and, yes, sometimes it will be because of that scar. But most of the time it'll be because that's how people get to know you and how they hold a conversation with you. By looking at you. Think about when you meet someone. Do you stare at her feet to try to learn what sort of person she is? I don't think so.'

The hands tightened their grip on Fiona's, and Sophie looked up, hope in her eyes. 'You believe that?'

Fiona nodded. 'I do.'

'What about the people who call me scar-face?'

'Take no notice of them. They're probably calling someone else fat or stupid or pimple-face. They're bullies, and you don't need their friendship anyway.'

'That's what Dad says.'

'See? Both of us can't be wrong.'

'Make that three of us,' growled Tom from behind her.

'That's the second time you've crept up on me.' So much for avoiding him.

'I don't creep. You didn't come back to the cottage.'

'I thought I'd do another patient round.' Twisting her head, she looked up at him, and immediately regretted her move.

His good looks caught at her, snagged her

attention. His strong chin had a tiny X-shaped scar under his right jaw that she hadn't seen before. His relaxed mouth made his bottom lip fuller, not stretched in annoyance as she'd seen so often since arriving. And suddenly she wanted to kiss those lips. Remembered kisses brought heady scents and tastes rushing back. She bit down on her bottom lip, trying to erase that thought. Tom's steady eyes met hers, giving her no clue to his thoughts. Her cheeks burned.

Tom grimaced, tightening his mouth. 'Sorry to interrupt you both, but, Fiona, you're needed.'

She dragged her gaze away from his face, shocked to find Sophie sitting before her, their hands still gripped together. How easy it would be to lean back against Tom's firm body and let go of all the tension eating away at her. To feel his arms go around her, holding her tight, would be like returning home.

'Who needs me?' Fiona croaked.

'One of the nurses called the cottage, thinking you'd be there. Shaun's getting fractious.'

Alarm brought Fiona straight back into focus. Fractious possibly meant an infection kicking in. Pushing off the bed, she said, 'See you in the morning, Sophie. And say ten times before you go to sleep tonight, "I am beautiful".'

Dashing along the corridor with Tom, she said, 'It seems too soon for an infection to be getting a grip. I've loaded him with antibiotics.'

'I read his chart. I'm not sure that's the problem. His temperature is thirty-seven point four.'

'Going up, then? The question is, why?' It had to be an infection. What else would cause Shaun's temperature to rise? 'Unless he's got an underlying illness.'

'Nothing his parents mentioned when filling in his admission forms,' Tom commented as he pushed open the door to Shaun's room and stood back to let Fiona enter.

Fiona plastered a smile on her face as she looked at the feverish boy. 'Hello, Shaun. How's your hand feeling?'

'It hurts.'

'The nurse gave him some analgesics with his dinner,' Shaun's mother commented.

Fiona read Shaun's latest observations. Why had his temperature risen? Not high enough for her to be too concerned yet, but rising body temperature in children was an early warning sign not to be ignored.

She checked his arm for reddened skin and found it normal, so there was no infection arising from the wound. But the lad was obviously feverish. His cheeks were a deep pink and his hair was damp on his forehead.

Fiona lifted Shaun's pyjama top. 'I'm going to check your tummy, Shaun. Have you got a tummy ache?'

'No.' Shaun's wary eyes stared at her.

No tenderness, no distended area. But as Fiona slipped the top back over Shaun's tummy, the boy rubbed his ear with his fist.

'Does your ear hurt?' Fiona asked, her mind quickly coming up with a list of causes.

Shaun nodded, and slid his thumb into his mouth.

Fiona examined Shaun's ears, then felt the glands in his neck and armpits. 'Open your mouth wide,' she instructed, and checked his throat. 'Have you had a sore throat lately?'

'Yes.'

'Why didn't you tell the nurse when you arrived yesterday?'

Shaun's worried gaze flicked across to his parents. 'I don't know.'

'Tom, do you want to look?' Fiona asked quietly,

but in a tone that left him in no doubt that he should.

While Tom examined the boy, Fiona flipped through Shaun's admission forms, clipped to the back of his medical notes hanging at the end of his bed.

Tom straightened and nodded to Fiona. 'I'll arrange bloods for a Paul Bunnell screen, and an EBV test.'

'Yes, I think we should.' Turning, Fiona asked, 'Mr and Mrs Elliott, how long has Shaun been complaining of a sore throat?'

'He said something about one last Monday, so I gave him cold mixture and he said it went away.' Reluctantly Mrs Elliott answered Fiona's question.

'You should've informed us before he had surgery.'

'Now, look here. What does it matter? It didn't affect his operation.' Mr Elliott's cheeks reddened. 'It's taken months for us to get the money together to come here. We weren't going to stay away for a bit of a cold.'

'We think he's got glandular fever. If he has, adding in the fact that he's underweight, then his recovery from today's surgery is going to be a lot slower than expected,' Fiona replied, barely keeping control of a sudden spurt of annoyance at these parents' attitude. They hadn't considered Shaun's overall health, or how it could affect other children in the hospital.

Tom put a hand on Fiona's arm, squeezed lightly in warning to take it quietly. 'I'll get one of the nurses to take some bloods and send them to the lab.'

Then Shaun's mother said the only thing that could appease Fiona.

'Please don't think too badly of us. Shaun gets such a hard time at school about his deformed hand that we'd do anything to make it near to normal again. Some days I have to drag him to school, and it breaks my heart to force him out of the car and in through the gates.'

'That's why I am a plastic surgeon,' Fiona muttered as she strode through the hospital with Tom. 'It's so hard on kids when their friends treat them differently.'

'Is that why you chose this specialty in the first place?' Tom peered down at her from his lofty height.

'I don't think I'd thought about it like that. The

delicate work and amazing results fascinated me at first. The need to help children overcome their problems so they can cope with a difficult world came later.'

'For me it's the whole picture. Helping all the family. Take Shaun's parents. They're distraught with worry over not being able to do enough for Shaun. You can see the hurt in their faces.'

Fiona struggled with her sadness. 'We know how that feels. We couldn't do anything to save Liam.'

'And we're doctors.'

They stopped and turned to face each other. They both reached a hand to the other, their fingers interlinked in a gentle squeeze before letting go.

'It was very hard to accept—all my training came down to absolutely nothing when I needed it the most.' Fiona heard the tremble in her voice.

'I think we both felt the same, and that's possibly when we began going our separate ways.' One of Tom's eyebrows lifted in query. 'That sense of being powerless seemed to flow over into every other part of our lives. No wonder we didn't know what to do about our marriage.

Does this answer your question about what went wrong?'

'I'm beginning to see it now. It was a horrific time.'

They walked slowly, quietly, each lost in thoughts of that time. Then Tom forced his mind back to the present and his patient.

'Mr and Mrs Elliot are struggling to pay for Shaun's surgery. They work every hour they can to raise the money. They've given up holidays and other things to see he gets the treatment he needs.'

'What about the public health system?' Fiona asked. 'He must qualify for that.'

'He was on the waiting list.' Tom felt a spurt of anger at the system. 'This case is classified non-urgent, so Shaun would have had to wait up to two years.'

Fiona flicked her gaze around to meet his. 'That's crazy. Think of the damage done from other children tormenting him all that time.'

'You don't have to tell me a thing.' Tom thought about Shaun's parents and the anguish he'd seen on their faces when he'd first met them. Shaun came before everything else in their lives. A picture filled his head of Shaun's dad, watching over his son early that morning before the boy was wheeled into Theatre. There had been tears in the man's eyes, tiredness dragging at his large muscle-bound body from working long, hard hours.

These parents were always there for their son. Not after their jobs. Not after helping their colleagues. *Before* those things. Unlike him. He'd always put his career first. He'd believed that being a paediatrician warranted his total dedication. But had he had to put it before Fiona and Liam?

If he had the time again would he do it differently? Definitely. He'd hug Fiona and Liam both every morning and every night. He'd be there every night.

A pager buzzed, jerking Tom back to the corridor and to Fiona, walking beside him. He flipped it off his belt and read the message, trying to refocus his mind away from the startling revelation he'd just had. 'Jarrod Harris wants to see me. I'm sure he's going to try and persuade me to let him go kayaking with the other haemophiliacs tomorrow, broken arm and all. Hard to have to dampen his spirit.'

'He's a great kid. What are you going to say?' Fiona asked.

'Would I be unreasonable if I said no?' His strides lengthened.

'What about a tandem kayak?'

'Water and a plaster cast don't mix well.'

'Clingwrap works wonders.' She glanced at him. 'If Jarrod hears about your reluctance to let him go he'll be trying to prove just how confident he really can be.'

'I don't doubt it.' He pushed through a door and held it open for her. As she slid past him, he added, 'You think I'm being unfair?'

'Jarrod came here for new experiences, remember?'

'I'm being responsible.' Or over-protective? Again?

'You're being too careful. Again.'

Same thing as over-protective.

She hadn't finished. 'Give the kid a chance to work this out for himself with a few well-chosen facts thrown in by you. He's old enough to be careful.'

'Yeah, right. Careful enough to fall out of a tree.'

'Do you buy cotton wool by the bale for these

kids?' The moment the words were out of her mouth she stepped back from him, her fingers touching her lips. 'I'm sorry. I shouldn't have said that. It's just that I feel for the boy and I want to put his case to you.'

Tom jammed his hands deep into his pockets. 'I'm sure Jarrod's quite capable of putting his own case, but since you have I'll approve his trip. That make you feel any better?' Actually, he liked that she cared enough to speak her mind.

'I could take him, if you'd lend me your vehicle. Then I can keep an eye on things.'

He held down a laugh. She wouldn't let up until she got what she wanted. 'Medical staff will already be there, but maybe you could drop him off and stay until he's on the water.'

He'd given in when he'd meant to keep Jarrod away from the river. The boy had come for fun, among other things, and who was he to stop him?

Fiona's smile felt like a reward.

Fiona watched Tom stride away. He didn't seemed too put out about Jarrod's trip. He'd changed his stance quite quickly. She'd had a moment of panic when she made that thoughtless comment about the cotton wool, but Tom had shrugged it off.

She turned towards the staffroom and the outside door that led to the cottage.

'Fiona?' Tom called softly.

Had he changed his mind again? 'Yes?'

'Let's have a meal in the village tonight. It would be fun to go out, and we really need to clear up a few issues.'

Go out with Tom? Yes, please. And sitting in a public place, surrounded by other people, would be far safer for her emotions than sharing his small kitchen, where tension sizzled between them.

'Fiona?' He took a step back towards her.

'Yes, that would be fine.' It would be marvellous. Her tummy did flips. Maybe they could relax with each other enough to talk openly about what went wrong. Then, maybe, she could move on and not look back.

Yeah, right. She was beginning to feel that she might never want to leave this place—and Tom.

'Then I'll see you later.' He glanced at his watch. 'It's ten to six. I'll be another hour yet.'

When she lifted her eyebrows in enquiry, he

added, 'The joys of being the boss. There's always plenty to do.'

'Then I'll find something to help out with until you're ready.'

But first she'd take a shower and change her clothes. Not that she'd brought anything more elegant than well-worn jeans and faded shirts, but a clean set would be an improvement. And no doubt surprise Tom.

Just before seven Tom went in search of Fiona. He'd had enough of paperwork, and as the thought of an evening with his ex-wife kept distracting his concentration he hadn't got as much done as he'd have liked. He couldn't help but wonder if he'd made a blunder, suggesting a meal out together. They might end up arguing and dragging up the pain from the past.

A shiver ran down his back despite the warmth of his merino jersey. Maybe they should discuss legalising their separation over dinner. A divorce. The next shiver rocked him. Was that what he really wanted? Wanted or not, it had to be the next phase in their relationship. There was nowhere else to go with it. They'd gone the distance, even though it had been a very short marriage, and it hadn't worked out. They were incompatible. Or were they? Strange, but he was enjoying having Fiona around the place—despite the sudden and difficult questions she occasionally threw at him. Face it: he had once loved Fiona deeply, so he had to have some residual feelings for her. But nothing as strong as he used to feel. Did it? He gulped. Surely he didn't still love her? He shook his head. No, that notion was way outside the square.

Loud giggles were coming from the games room as he neared the door. Peering in, he felt his breath catch in his throat. Sprawled on the carpet, with four little children crawling all over and around her, lay his wife. She was telling a story about a lion, interspersing the tale with loud, slightly odd roars that sent the kids off into fresh bouts of giggles.

As he watched, Tom's heart clenched with a fierce longing. A longing for what he didn't have. Children. His own family. A future beyond the walls of this hospital. He'd made this place his whole life, and now that life felt empty. There was more for him out there, and he wanted a slice of whatever was going.

He gasped. Where the hell had *that* come from?

This place kept him fully occupied. There were no spare hours for anything else. Anyone else.

But something's missing.

His eyes followed Fi as she played with the youngsters, a full and genuine smile on her lovely face. His heart rolled over. He hadn't seen that particular smile for a very long time and it made him feel soft and warm inside. Did he want that slice of life to be with her?

Liz, a nurse, spoke quietly beside him. 'The children adore Fiona. She's a natural with them.'

'Kids have always been attracted to Fiona for her larger-than-life personality.' Which had quietened down somewhat.

'She certainly empathises with them.'

'You're right. Each of these children has been admitted today for plastic surgery tomorrow, yet here they are having pure fun, with no sign of fear or nerves about their operations. Fiona's treating each child with so much care, being gentle with them, so they're building up trust with her.'

He continued to watch Fiona. Absorbed in the story and the game, she seemed unaware of her appearance, and oblivious to the mess her hair was getting into as one little girl grabbed handfuls to use as a mane. Another difference caught his eye. She'd changed her shirt, probably in preparation for their meal in town. Now that shirt was wrinkled and crushed.

Should he make a sound, let Fiona know he was here? The moment she sensed his presence the spell would be broken and his heartbeat could return to normal.

It took some effort getting used to this new image of the woman he'd been married to. Where had the glamorous little black dresses gone? It astonished him that she hadn't packed one for the week. One? A case full. His lips curved into a smile. Fi. It had been so long. He'd missed her.

The wonder on her face as she lifted a little girl above her head transported him back down the years to when Liam had been only weeks old. He'd often seen a similar, but more intense look on Fi's face as she'd cradled their son in her arms. He blinked, but the picture didn't go away. He could see her breastfeeding Liam, awestruck at caring for her child in the most basic of ways. She was born to be a mother.

Why had it happened to them? Why had their son gone? He gulped, swallowed a lump, surreptitiously wiped his eyes. He'd never get an answer to that question.

'Tom, come and join us. I need some help with these lion cubs.' Fiona caught and held his gaze above the children.

He shook his head, trying desperately to get his emotions under control.

'Tom.' Her voice was low and insistent even as she tickled another child. 'We need a father lion.' Her hand reached out towards him.

'No. You carry on. You're doing a great job.'

'Come on. We'll do this together.'

And he understood she wasn't only referring to the game. She'd read his pain so easily.

Tom grimaced as he approached the laughing group. He'd been caught in a bad moment. But he tried to pick up on the infectious good humour of the children. 'I don't do a good roar.' Like he'd ever tried.

'Give it a go.' Fiona touched his shoulder.

His first attempt got stuck behind the lump in his throat. But one look from Fiona and he was down on his hands and knees, trying again. Astonishingly, he managed some semblance of a roar this time. So now he was a male lion, teaching his cubs to hunt. The things this woman could get him to do.

'The louder the roar the better, according to these cubs.' Fiona grinned, sending his heart to do that funny clenching thing it had been doing on and off for hours.

'Great. What will my staff think of me rolling around on the floor like a complete dork?' He smiled back.

'That you're not as toffee-nosed as they thought.' Her wink took the sting out her words.

'My nose is not made of toffee,' he told a little girl who was looking at him all perplexed. 'Dr Fiona doesn't always talk a lot of sense.'

'She's funny,' said one of Fiona's young admirers.

And clever, and exciting, and warm, and very loving.

The lion roared.

CHAPTER SIX

'IT's good to meet you, Fiona,' Craig said as he set his menu aside. 'Tom has mentioned you occasionally when we've tried to delve into his dark and secret past.'

'Yes, I did feature in it for a while.' Fiona's smile looked tentative as she glanced at Tom. 'Secret, huh?'

'Craig's exaggerating. He likes to embellish stories.' Tom sighed. Of course his friends would want to ask questions. They knew he'd once been married, and had lost a son. When he'd learned that Fiona had offered to fill in the week for Jerome they'd been the first people he'd told.

From the moment he and Fiona had entered the restaurant and seen Craig and Kerry being seated he'd known they'd be expected to join them. He'd sensed Fiona's disappointment at having their talk postponed, but he'd felt nothing but relief.

'Call me nosey.' Craig grinned. 'I like knowing all about my friends, and Tom isn't very forthcoming at times.'

Tom saw Fiona glance at him knowingly. 'That's probably because when we were together I did enough talking for both of us. He couldn't get a word in.'

Fiona was defending him? What was more, it was about his inability to spill the beans about things that mattered most to him. Was his brain playing tricks? He checked his wine glass but it was still full. His hand moved of its own volition to briefly touch her elbow.

Kerry asked her, 'Where'd you meet? Across a bed in a ward somewhere?'

'Almost. Tom was in his final year of specialist training and I was on intern rotation through the paediatric ward. I had my hands full with a frightened three-year-old, kicking and screaming her lungs out. Tom rescued me.'

'Sounds like when Craig and I met—except he's a vet and I took my spaniel to him after she'd been struck by a car. I was freaking out and totally panicked about my dog, and the vet just calmed me down with a few words.' Kerry grinned. 'Then he started telling jokes and making me smile, all the time treating Polly with such tenderness I knew straight away I had to get to know this man.'

Fiona smiled at Tom. 'No jokes on the job with Tom. He tended to be quite serious, but great with junior doctors. Plus every female in the hospital wanted to get to know him.'

Kerry laughed. 'They still do.'

'That's enough. What's everyone having for dinner?' Tom felt mildly uncomfortable. He'd expected criticism from Fiona, not compliments.

'The fish and salad for me,' Fiona answered.

'What? Not the creamy pasta with chicken?' She'd used to eat pasta at every opportunity.

'Too rich for me these days.' She looked almost sad.

Tom grinned. 'No wonder you've slimmed down so much.' He'd always loved her soft curves; thinner though she was now, she was still beautiful, but faint hollows in her cheeks made her look a little tired, vulnerable.

'That's not when I lost the weight…' Fiona's voice trailed away as she nodded at someone behind him.

Tom looked up to see the waitress hovering at his elbow. As she took their orders he wondered what Fiona had been about to say. Had she been ill at some time since she'd left him? Did that explain the physical changes in her? A trickle of fear set his skin on edge. Fi ill? Please, no. Not that. He knew she couldn't abide people discussing their health unless it was in a patient-to-doctor situation. She always said she had enough medical talk at work not to want to hear her friends discussing their ailments socially. The same applied to herself. Not that he'd ever known her to be ill. She'd always said she didn't have time for bad health.

'Your work with Global Health sounds so exotic compared to Hanmer Springs,' Kerry said

'You think so?' Fiona looked surprised. 'From the little I've seen, this place is paradise. Except for the temperatures.'

'At least you've stopped shivering,' Tom noted. 'You'll feel the cold when we go back outside if you don't take your jacket off in here.'

'I'll borrow yours and put it over the top of mine.' She caught his eye, and suddenly they both smiled, then spoke at the same time.

'Like I always did.'

'You stole my jackets or coats whenever we were out. And they were way too big for you.'

And when he'd put one of those jackets on later

there'd always be a hint of Fiona's perfume on them. For weeks after she'd left him he'd wear a jacket just to have something of her with him. Eventually the scent had faded, disappeared, and he'd been left only with memories.

Craig and Kerry's laughter broke through his reminiscing, drew him back to listen to Fiona telling amusing anecdotes about her experiences overseas. She continued to enthral them all so that dinner passed quickly.

Tom sipped his wine and smiled internally. Tonight had turned out to be fun. Everyone was relaxed, Fiona had been entertaining, and he'd stopped worrying about what she might want to talk about with him. Yes, this took him back to nights out in the early days of their marriage.

Just then the woman in his mind looked up and he smiled at her. She gave him a slow wink. His gut clenched. In the old days when they were out with other people that wink could have meant, *Aren't we having fun?* or it could have been saying *Isn't this so boring? Let's get out of here.* Tonight he figured she meant they were having fun. Tonight he'd sit back and continue to enjoy his evening, and pretend they were like any other normal couple.

Kerry spooned sugar into her coffee, saying thoughtfully, 'I can see why you'd want to go back after your leave's finished.'

Tom's hand stilled on his cup. Did she want to go back? Of course she would. Anyone listening to her for the last half-hour would know full well how much she'd loved what she'd been doing. Her face had come alive as she'd talked about the people she'd helped and the places she'd worked in. Fiona had found her niche in life. Once Fiona became passionate about something she didn't let go. Not easily, anyway.

She had let go of their marriage. But easily? No, they'd both struggled to make it work. They'd failed each other because neither had known what to do about the dreadful situation they'd found themselves in.

Fiona explained to Kerry, 'I'm not sure what I'm going to do next. The last three years have been wonderful, but now that I'm back home I'm starting to realise there are so many things I've been missing. Friends, family…' She hesitated.

What family? Her father? Her mother had died before she and Tom had married. Him? Had she missed him at all?

'A sense of belonging,' she concluded.

This was something new. The old Fi had slotted in anywhere by dint of making everything around her hers.

Her eyes slid in his direction. 'I know I've only been here a little over twenty-four hours, but already I can see what you're doing at the hospital is awesome.'

Warmth crept over him. It felt good to know she approved of what he was doing. 'Thanks, but it's not just about me.'

'True. He needs the rest of us to make tea and coffee and keep the cookie jar in his office full,' quipped Kerry.

Craig leaned closer to Tom and spoke quietly, 'Think you can persuade her to stay?'

'I wouldn't have a clue.' Did he even want her to stay? In what capacity? Specialist—yes. He could always put her skills to good use. But how would he cope having her living in the same small village twenty-four-seven? And why was he even considering the idea? He didn't believe in second chances.

In Theatre the next morning Fiona told Kerry, 'You can bring Megan round now. I'm done.'

Snapping her latex gloves as she tugged them

off, Fiona looked down at the little girl and smiled. The skin graft to repair a nasty burn from a log falling out of a firebox onto Megan's leg had gone very well. 'There you go, my little lion cub. That leg should look a lot better in a few days.'

'I heard about a bit of an African scene in the games room last night,' Kerry commented as she read printouts. 'Apparently our boss makes a terrific roar, and looks quite sexy on his hands and knees with his backside pointing skyward.'

'Who's been blabbing?' Fiona asked, amused that the staff had found Tom's participation in the game she'd made up worthy of gossip.

'Megan told me all about it while I prepped her. Not the bit about Tom looking sexy. That came from Liz. Of course I asked for all the finer details. Seems you weave a good yarn too.'

'I've had plenty of practice.' Fiona tried not to think about Tom's backside—for all of two seconds. His derrière was *very* sexy. She'd always found him physically attractive. Studying him now, seeing the little crinkles at the corners of his mouth, the maturity in his face wrought by tragedy and the passing years, she still found him attractive. Very attractive. *Stop. Back up.* Wrong place, wrong time to be thinking like this, and far too late to do anything about it.

Tom looked at them both and shook his head despairingly. 'Surely you two have got something better to talk about than my rear end?'

'Can't think of anything.' Kerry grinned.

'We could discuss the feeding habits of tadpoles instead.' Fiona wiggled her hand in the air between them. 'Not half as much fun. Tadpoles don't react.'

Tom rolled his eyes. 'You haven't changed a bit, Fiona Saville.'

Yes. She wanted to punch the air. Saville. He'd done it—used her married name—his name. And, judging from the unperturbed look on his face, he hadn't even realised. But she shouldn't be getting excited. It was only a name. It was also one small step towards reconciling the past. Wasn't that what she wanted?

Tom came in through his front door that night and stopped, a stunned expression on his face.

Fiona waved at him. 'You've a fantastic music collection,' she called over the heavy beat of one of his jazz CDs, then sashayed across to turn the volume down a tad. Her hips rolled and her feet tip-tapped of their own accord as the rhythm flowed through her body. She loved jazz, and hadn't heard much in years.

Tom rolled his eyes and went to turn the volume down further. 'I can't believe I didn't hear that in my office.'

She laughed. 'Don't exaggerate.'

'I didn't think I was.' Tom seemed to be watching her crazy dance movements, a surprised look in his eyes. Did he still fancy her? Was he dredging up old memories? Her mouth dried. *Don't go there.*

She stopped moving around, thinking it would be wise to go back to finishing the meal preparation. 'I've made a chicken casserole. I hope that's okay?'

'It's more than okay. I wasn't looking forward to cooking tonight.' He shucked off his jacket and hung it neatly over the back of a chair. 'It's beginning to snow.'

'Guess that's what's melting off your jacket onto the floor.'

Turning down the fire's air flow, Tom placed the chair on the hearth, near enough to dry his jacket but not so close that it might scorch. 'It'll dry quickly enough. It's very warm in here. That's some fire you've managed to get going.'

'Another of my new skills. The nights were extremely cold in the desert, and I had to learn to light a fire or freeze.' Looking after the fire had been Tom's job in winter, just as it had been Fiona's to buy the groceries as Tom had been inclined to come home with bags of totally useless gadgets that the supermarkets hocked off cheaply.

'Feel like a glass of wine before dinner?' he asked.

'There's a Sauvignon Blanc in the fridge. Hope that's to your taste?'

'Perfect. I'll get it, and you can tell me how Jarrod enjoyed his kayaking trip.'

She'd driven the boy to the river at lunchtime. 'He had a wonderful time. I envied him.'

'I bet you did. I'm surprised you didn't join him.' Tom frowned. 'I hope he was sensible.'

'Jarrod was very careful not to knock his arm, or any part of his body, for that matter. He's very mature about his haemophilia.'

'Apart from yesterday's mishap.'

'Granted. But can you really blame him? Today he enjoyed doing things other people his age do.

He didn't have a hair-raising trip; he was quite sedate for such a lively lad. I had fun watching his pleasure.'

'Very sensible for a thirty-five-year-old woman who has a history of partaking in dangerous sports,' Tom teased as he handed her a glass of the wine.

'I have far more respect for my life and limbs these days.'

'So you intimated earlier.' He nodded, smiling at her, a full megawatt smile. The sort that used to melt her bones. Still did. 'I confess to noticing some changes.' He stared at her for a long moment, before turning to fold up a newspaper lying on the table and put it away in a drawer.

She gulped her wine. Careful. She and alcohol didn't mix well. Too much and she was inclined to get stroppy. Neither of them needed that. For her, one glass was too much. So, putting her drink aside, she went to the oven to check on the casserole. Next she put rice in the boiling water, before saying, 'You've got these haemophiliac patients and their families staying here for a week.'

'No way. Once a month we have a different group in. Kids with arthritis, leukaemia, diabetes—you name it. There's a medical component to the week, with specialists, therapists and social workers to talk with the children. But the major reason for these weeks is to give them the opportunity to socialise with others dealing with the same conditions.'

She noted he'd said 'dealing with' rather than 'suffering from' the same conditions. It was an important, positive approach which would go a long way to bolstering his patients' confidence and their outlook on life.

'The kids you've got staying now seem to be having a fantastic time—one broken arm notwithstanding.'

'It's always like this. The good things, I mean.' He raised an eyebrow at her. 'Okay, I admit to the fun thing, and that's how it should be. I've been very lucky that the local adventure companies have come on board and offered their facilities and staff for these kids to use. They all give their time and equipment for free. I think they get as much enjoyment out of it as the children.'

Tom began setting the table for dinner, lining up the cutlery against the placemats. Fiona smiled. Tonight she'd forego teasing him by moving the forks.

His movements were smooth and controlled,

but his hands caught her imagination. Strong, with long, tapered fingers, she knew they could be as tough as a vice when needed, or as gentle as a butterfly landing on her skin. Her eyes closed over memories of that soft touch on her body, touching here, touching there, turning her so hot she'd always been surprised she hadn't burned up.

'Fiona? Are you all right?' Real concern shadowed his voice.

Her eyes snapped open and she turned back to the stove, hoping he didn't see her embarrassment at being caught daydreaming about him…about them.

'Yes, I'm fine. Bit tired, I guess.'

Any further comments he might have made were lost in the clatter of banging pot lids and dishes being laid on the bench so she could serve their dinner. She put her pink cheeks down to the heat from the oven when she'd removed the casserole.

'Guess it has been a long day for you.'

'No, today was easy compared to the hours we were doing in Pakistan. Over there we tended to work every hour available because of the never-ending stream of patients. Besides, we had very little else to do in the way-out places Global Health sent us to.'

'No sightseeing, then?'

'Only on our few days off, and even then it wasn't always easy to get transport.' Fiona placed the dishes of food in the centre of the table and sat down opposite Tom. Just like in the days of their marriage. Or those of them when they'd both been at home at the same time, and Tom hadn't been racing back to the hospital for an extra shift.

Tom lifted the lid of the casserole dish and sniffed appreciatively. 'Chicken and asparagus. One of my favourites.'

Too late, Fiona realised the mistake she'd made. Now he'd be thinking she was trying to win him over and keep him happy. Maybe subconsciously, that was exactly what she'd intended when she'd popped into the small supermarket to get chicken on the way back from the river.

'I mostly used what I could find in your cupboards. It's nothing special,' she stuttered.

Tom stole a mouthful straight from the dish before piling his plate high. 'It's great.' His tongue licked his lips clean.

'Glad you like it,' she mumbled, toying with the

rice she'd spooned onto her plate. Her appetite had disappeared; sitting across from Tom was proving too hard. It felt as though she'd slipped back into the life she'd known before they'd started having difficulties. It had been a life she'd loved.

It had been Tom she'd loved!

She had enjoyed every aspect of their marriage, even their little differences. That was what had made their marriage so unpredictable and fun—especially the making up. No making up now, though. Their differences had become too huge.

'Here, let me give you some of this.' Tom served a large spoonful of chicken onto her plate.

It was obvious he didn't have any problems with his appetite. Neither should she. She muttered, 'Thanks,' and began eating, at first chewing every mouthful slowly, trying to swallow it. But as Tom ate and chatted about his hospital the tension in her stomach began to ease, and she started enjoying her meal and Tom's company in a relaxed, friendly kind of way.

She spoke between mouthfuls. 'I met Connor earlier. He told me you pay him to do some jobs around the place.'

'His mother is struggling to bring up two kids on her own.'

'And this is your way of helping her?'

Tom had finished a second helping of casserole and was now sipping his wine, staring somewhere over her shoulder. 'He reminded me of my best friend at that age. Billy. His family had no money either, so he had a newspaper round to buy school books and lunch.'

Tom had never mentioned a friend from his childhood. 'This friend, where is he now?'

'He had an accident—a fatal one.'

'That's awful.' She shuddered.

Tom's eyes were bleak. 'He used my bike for his paper round. One day he was late, and I'd been oiling the bike chain. There was a long hill from our place to the store where he picked up his papers.' Tom swallowed hard.

Oh, no. Fiona got up and crossed to stand beside him, her arm over his shoulders. 'Go on.'

'I'd spilled oil on the brake pads. A car came around the corner at the same moment as Billy reached it. He didn't survive. We were both ten at the time. I missed him incredibly.'

Under her hand Fiona felt the shudder passing through Tom. She rubbed gentle circles over his tense muscles. 'You never told me this.' She might have understood him better if he had. It seemed he'd left out all the really important aspects of his life. How many other things had he kept from her?

'I never, ever talked about it to anyone. I wanted to in the beginning, but my parents always said it would be best to forget the whole incident. They told me I'd get over it quicker that way.' He sighed and twisted around to look at her. 'My family were never any good at talking.'

'I wish I'd known.'

The scraping sound Tom's chair made on the tile floor as he stood up screeched across her brain. The hand that touched, held her chin, felt gentle as it tipped her head back so that she looked into the deep, sad pools of Tom's eyes. 'So do I, but we can't undo the past now.'

'I might have acted differently—might not have given you such a hard time for not talking to me.' But he had talked to her tonight, ever so slightly—about his friend. About something that had hurt him badly as a child. And still hurt him.

He shifted his head slowly from side to side.

'Don't go there, Fi.' Sadness puckered his mouth.

She blinked, forced herself to look away. Years ago she'd done a lifetime's worth of crying, had been dry-eyed for nearly five years now. That was why she shouldn't be thinking of wanting Tom back. Everyone knew that once you got into a relationship with anyone—husband, lover, child, even a friend—there were going to be tears somewhere along the way.

'You're right, of course.' She covered his hand with hers, felt his warmth.

'For years I blamed myself for Billy's death. It's only recently I've accepted that more than one thing went wrong that day to culminate in a tragic accident.'

'Recently?' Since Liam's death? She wanted to ask him, but she was afraid he might withdraw from her again and she didn't want that. Not now, when he'd actually spoken to her about something so important to him.

Right now she was desperate to hold him in her arms and kiss away the pain in those beautiful eyes that she'd fallen in love with such a long time ago.

What held her back? Was she afraid he'd push

her away? And if he did? At least she'd have tried. She stepped closer to him, and reached to touch his face. Her fingers moved of their own accord, tracing his mouth, reliving the memories of the curve of his chin, his cheekbones. She stretched up on her toes and touched his lips with hers. He trembled under her touch, made no move to draw away—or nearer.

She swallowed, pressed her lips closer, savoured him. It wasn't enough. She slid her tongue across his lips, shivered in the heady mix of wine and Tom.

His hands caught her upper arms, pushed her just far enough away from him to break the contact with her mouth. 'Fiona, don't. We— This isn't right.'

Her whisper croaked through her closed throat. 'I've wanted to kiss you ever since I arrived.'

Tom stared at her, his mouth softening before he groaned, hauled her against him, and crushed his mouth to hers. A hard, demanding kiss that touched every cell in her body. A kiss that caressed fires that had been smothered for far too long.

She leaned into him, pressed as close as possible, flattening her breasts against his chest. And she wasn't close enough. She pushed her thighs against his. Her skin crackled with longing. Her mouth was filled with Tom, his tongue seeking, exploring, tasting. She tasted and explored right back. She'd come home. They belonged together.

Then abruptly Tom was setting her away from him, leaving her blinking like a rabbit in headlights. What had happened? 'Tom?'

'Sorry, we shouldn't be doing this.' His hands dragged down his cheeks as he stumbled backwards. 'There's too much between us to be even thinking about getting close and personal.'

'I should be the one to apologise. I started it.' What had she been thinking of, kissing Tom? She hadn't been thinking at all. There lay the problem.

Tom snatched up his jacket and all but ran out of the room, muttering over his shoulder, 'I need to catch up on some paperwork.'

Paperwork? Fiona shrugged. Right, whatever. It was probably for the best. Their kiss had begun to really crank up into something she wasn't so sure she'd have been able to stop if they'd carried on much longer. Would they have ended up making love? And then what? Tom had made it plain he wasn't interested in rekindling their relationship. That hadn't been her intention either when she'd first arrived.

It still wasn't.

Just do the job and go away, she chanted in her head. Do the job and go away. Forget trying to put the past to rest. It wasn't going to lie down, so she might as well leave it be.

But her heart was aching.

Tom kicked at a clump of snow on his front step. What he really needed was to get his head read. How could he have kissed Fiona? How could he have let her get even that close to him?

Hold up. She'd kissed him first. A sweet kiss that had sneaked in under his ribs and tickled his heart. Yeah, and he'd been quick to run with it, deepen it, until all his resolve to stay clear of Fiona had just disappeared as fast as the snap of his fingers. He smacked his forehead with his palm. How could he have taken her in his arms and put his lips to hers? Because that first kiss had fried his brain cells, had made him feel as though he'd finally found what he'd been looking for ever since Fiona had left him. That sense of being in the right place with the right person, the one woman who had been able to get beneath his skin and make him feel like he belonged, had returned as quickly as it took to start a kiss.

Stomping along the path heading away from the hospital, he tried to squash the feeling that he was losing control over his emotions. He searched for the inner strength that he always applied when the hurt and anger and bewilderment he felt around Fiona threatened to topple his world, but tonight he couldn't put those feelings back in their place. He wanted her! Badly! She hummed in his blood. She stirred him so deeply it frightened him. His pulse thumped in his head.

He wanted to throw caution aside and race back into the cottage where he could lift Fiona against his chest. He ached to replace his lips on hers, to taste her sweetness again, to feel her melt against him. To claim her.

His legs stretched out as his pace increased, taking him further from temptation. He would never be that vulnerable again.

This dashing out of the cottage after dinner was becoming a habit. Fiona stared at the shut door and ran her shaking fingers across her swollen lips. But at least tonight they'd been kissing, not arguing.

But she shouldn't have kissed him. Instead of easing the situation between them the tension had been racked up. She'd swear he'd been as shaken as she had. She'd felt his body quiver as their kiss lengthened. She'd tasted the heat of his tongue, smelt the increased maleness of his desire. Tom had wanted her as much as she'd wanted him.

She reached for the glass of wine she'd put aside before dinner. What did it matter if she got a little bit cranky now? Tom wasn't here to notice. Oh, no, he'd dashed off to work.

Just like the good old times. Avoiding the situation. Not stopping to talk about what had happened between them.

Wise up, Fiona. Tom hasn't changed as much as you'd hoped.

CHAPTER SEVEN

AFTER cleaning up the kitchen Fiona went to bed. Burrowed under the blankets, with the pillow tucked down around her neck, she tried to keep warm and hold the world at bay. Twice she nearly clambered out of bed to go and find Tom so she could be with him, to see if there was anything she could help with. Twice she chickened out, not wanting to upset him any further than that kiss seemed to have done.

Finally she dozed off—only to be woken by the phone ringing. If Tom had returned he'd get it. It would be for him anyway. Shivering, she pushed her head out of the cocoon of blankets and listened.

It continued to ring, sounding insistent in the quiet cottage. What if something had happened to one of her patients? Groaning, she crawled out and, grabbing her jersey, ran to the kitchen. Then stopped. The ringing came from inside Tom's bedroom.

Someone must want him badly. The ringing persisted. Inside Tom's bedroom door she ran her hand over the wall, searching for the light switch. Yellow light flooded the room, and she blinked. The phone lay on his bed. Pressing 'talk' she held it to her ear, only to hear a click and the dial tone. Typical. She tossed the phone down.

Shivering, she tugged her jersey over her head and down her tee shirt. Then she looked around Tom's room.

Her lips twisted into a small smile as she saw his immaculately made bed. Her fingers reached for his pillow, lingering where his head might have lain the night before. Picking it up, she clutched it to her breast, inhaling Tom.

Over the edge of the pillow she looked around. A collection of black and white photos hung on the wall above his bed. All landscapes. He had a natural eye for balance and a real sense of the dramatic. None of the photos were familiar to her.

'At least he's still doing his photography.'

Fiona spoke out loud in an attempt to dispel the guilt she felt at invading his privacy.

'But all these photos are impersonal. What happened to that wonderful collection of candid shots you took of people at the market, on the beach, everywhere?'

On his bedside table a photo frame lay face down. Automatically she lifted it and turned it over.

A sharp cry stung the night. Her cry.

In the deceptively simple photo Tom had captured her love for their baby as she held him against her breast. Liam. She remembered when the photo had been taken. Three days before he died.

Raw pain sliced her, tearing through her body like a hot knife through butter. Her knees jarred as she fell to the floor, still clutching the photo. She couldn't take her eyes off the picture. She hadn't looked at a photo of Liam for five years. Not since the day she'd made up her mind to put the past behind her and try to make a new life. Until then, every time she'd looked at Liam's picture the guilt had gnawed at her, driving her almost insane.

Rocking on her knees, she stared at her son, willing him alive, knowing that was impossible. She drank him in. He had been gurgling contentedly, his tiny fist waving at Tom behind the camera. Now he should be running around with an abundance of energy, looking like his dad with that beautiful smile that tore through her.

'I'm sorry, baby. I loved you so much and I let you die.'

The ache in her throat prevented her swallowing. Her jaw hurt as she fought the pain. Her eyes burned from unshed tears as she folded over her thighs. Her baby.

'Fiona? Oh, my God. How did you find that? Oh, sweetheart, what are you doing in here?' Tom had come back, was kneeling before her, scooping her into his arms. 'You weren't ever meant to see that photo. I knew it would break your heart. I didn't leave it lying around deliberately. Believe me.'

She sagged against him. All the energy had poured out of her. 'It—it's like starting o-over,' she stuttered around the ball in her throat. *Tom had called her sweetheart.* 'As though the last six years haven't m-meant a th-thing.'

'Shh,' Tom soothed, gently smoothing her hair away from her face. He wriggled around and leant back against his bed, lifting her onto his thighs.

'I—' She hiccupped, swallowed, started again.

'I shouldn't have come here. It's my own fault, but I thought I was strong enough.'

Tom slid his arms around her. 'There's no avoiding the fact we had a son between us. He's going to be there, in our hearts, in our very souls, for ever. It hurts and always will.' His words almost a whisper, his light breaths lifting strands of her hair.

Now that they'd started, her tears continued in a flood, streaming down her cheeks, splashing onto Tom's arms around her middle. 'You know, you never admitted as much back then.'

'Just looking at you reminds me of Liam.'

Fiona gasped as pain again lanced her, stabbing her stomach, her lungs, her heart. Liam. Their baby. She blurted, 'He had your curls, your generous mouth.'

'Your blue eyes, your fair hair.' Tom's chin dropped on to the top of her head, and his hands caught together around her midriff. 'He was so tiny.'

'He was five months old.' Of course he was tiny. And beautiful. And perfect. And she still missed him as though it had happened yesterday.

'Have you moved on at all?' Tom asked.

'No one forgets their child, Tom. I carry him in

my heart everywhere I go. I think of him dozens of times a day.'

Tom's head lifted. 'You seem whole.'

Oh, Tom. 'I don't often feel it.'

'But you do feel it sometimes?'

Did he blame her for Liam's death? It had been horrendous when Liam died, but years had gone by—Tom had to have made peace with himself.

She tried explaining. 'Sometimes, when I'm helping people, especially children, I know a sense of peace for a little while. Those times have helped me get through some of the bad hours.' She reached out a hand to his, her touch light against his fingers. Under her palm his heart thundered, and a yearning to embrace him, to soothe away the pain in his face, uncurled deep inside her.

Under her bottom she felt his thighs tense and his arms tighten their hold, then he relaxed. Was that a kiss on the top of her head? Heaven knew, she needed one. A real one, soft on the lips, big on comfort. Did Tom need one, too?

She raised her head, her mouth reaching for his. His lips were warm over hers. Their mouths blended together. Joining their pain, sharing their loss, seeking and giving solace. Not the kind of kiss that friends exchanged, but not one of passionate lovers either. Nothing like their earlier one.

It *was* what they needed.

She leaned into him, seeking shelter from her life as it had become. And her tongue slipped between his lips, tasted him. Again her head swam with memories. Tender memories. Hot memories. Her spine tingled. And then Tom's mouth was no longer gentle but demanding. Her spirits soared as she returned his kisses.

This was what she remembered. The meltdown. The sheer delight in kissing Tom, in being kissed by him. She was floating, getting warmer by the second. Her body responded like a drought-stricken plain—hot sensations flooding over her, washing away the long, lonely nights.

A groan escaped Tom's lips.

She blinked. Paused mid-kiss. What was she doing? Setting herself up for more heartbreak? There could be no future in this. One stolen kiss, or more, wouldn't solve a thing. For either of them. She leaned backwards, slowly pulling her lips from Tom's beautiful mouth.

'Fi?' Slowly Tom opened his eyes, looking

startled to find her watching him. 'Oh, hell, I'm sorry. So much for the talk I gave myself half an hour ago.'

He lifted her off his thighs and scrambled upright. Leaning down, he offered her a hand, tugged her up onto her feet. 'I don't know what to say,' he added softly, shaking his head in a bemused fashion.

Fiona reached a hand to his face, touched him lightly. 'It takes two, Tom.'

His answering smile was brief and filled with guilt. 'Sure.'

Fiona bent down to retrieve the photo that had started this. She studied it, her heart squeezing. 'I guess all mothers think their baby is gorgeous, but Liam really was.'

'I think all mothers say exactly that. Of course he was gorgeous. We wouldn't have been normal parents if we hadn't been blinded to any imperfections.'

She swung around. 'Imperfections? What do you mean?'

Tom lifted his hands and shrugged, a warm smile teasing his lips. 'See? You defend him instantly. That's great. And anyway, he *was* perfect. Apart from the sleepless nights he gave us.'

Relaxing again, she placed a kiss on Liam's head and placed the photo upright on Tom's dressing table. 'I miss you so much. Every day.'

'You're talking to Liam, right?'

Fiona blinked. Gazed at her son. Yes. She was. But had she been talking to Tom as well? Not intentionally. But truthfully? The breath she hadn't realised she held oozed past her lips, lips now swollen from Tom's kisses. Yes, she'd missed Tom every single day and night since the moment she'd left him. Even during the years she'd spent fully focused on medicine and helping others there had been a feeling of loss that she couldn't entirely pin on Liam.

Turning to Tom, she murmured, 'Of course.'

The chilly room caused her to shiver. Gathering up the quilt folded over a chair, she wrapped herself in it and curled up on the end of the bed. She really should move out into the kitchen or the lounge, but she couldn't bring herself to leave that photo just yet.

Her voice wobbled when she said, 'Tell me about what you did, where you went, after I left town. I mean, how did you get from working in the paediatric department at Auckland Hospital to opening your own hospital in the South Island?'

The bed dipped as Tom sat at the opposite end and shuffled his backside up onto the pillows. Leaning against the headboard, he clasped his hands behind his head and gazed at the ceiling. 'I think the idea began bubbling away at the back of my mind as I worked with children at Auckland. I saw so many of them needing to get together with other kids coping with similar problems. Their parents needed that sort of contact too. But after we split up I first took a position at Christchurch Hospital.'

'The one city you always said you'd never live in.'

'I needed to get out of Auckland for a while. Quite frankly, I didn't care where I went, so when a job came up in Christchurch I applied.' He looked wistful. 'I loved working in Auckland, but I couldn't focus any more. I figured a change would do the trick.'

'Did it?' It hadn't for her. Not initially, anyway.

He lowered his eyes to look at her. 'Yes and no. I immersed myself in work, but that wasn't enough to fill in the long, empty hours when I returned to my flat at night. So I began toying with my dream of setting up a specialist hospital. Almost overnight the dream grew into reality. Sometimes I thought it had become a monster, but it did keep me busy and the images of Liam and you at bay.'

'Are you happy, Tom?'

'There are degrees of happiness. Considering what happened to me…us…yes, I think I am content.' A shadow crossed his eyes.

'You don't sound convinced.' What was missing from his life? A woman? Family? Of course that had to be the answer. He came from a good family, and he'd always wanted to emulate that with her and Liam. The void in his heart would be huge.

'Let's drop this, Fiona.'

'No, let's not. We've dropped too many hard issues in the past when if we'd worked our way through them instead we might never have separated.' *Steady,* she warned herself. *Don't get uptight.* Drawing a rough breath, she squeezed out the words she'd needed to say for a long time. 'Tom, I'm sorry for leaving that day, for the way I just up and went. Driving through that red light and crashing the car was the last straw.

Suddenly it seemed imperative I get away and try to straighten my head out. At the time I wasn't going for good, just for however long it took to sort myself out. Unfortunately it took a lot longer than I'd ever imagined.' Years longer.

He reached for her hand, gripped it between his, his warmth seeping into her. 'I should've tried harder to hear what you were really telling me. I couldn't understand you at the time. It seemed that everything I tried to do for you was wrong. The paediatric unit became the one place where I did get things right, and so I spent more and more time there. When you left I knew I'd failed you by not being able to help you through your grief.'

'Tom, all I wanted from you was for you to tell me your feelings. Now, after hearing about Billy, I understand why you couldn't talk. You'd been brought up to hold everything in.'

He dropped her hand as though it was poisonous. 'My son gone and you wanted to know how I *felt*?' Pain deepened his voice, darkened his grey eyes to coal. His hands were clenched on his thighs.

'Of course I knew.' She took both fists in her hands. 'But I needed you to share those feelings.

I told you about my pain and I got nothing back. We created Liam together, through our love. We were together when he came into the world. But we mourned him separately.'

His fists opened, clasped both her hands. 'I thought I was helping you by being outwardly strong. I wanted to be your anchor, carry your grief as well as mine.'

'Was I truly so selfish that you thought I wouldn't help you?'

With one hand he brushed an errant strand of hair off her face. 'No. You have to understand that's the only way I knew how to cope. By focusing on your grief I avoided my own.'

'You seemed so remote. I'd lost not only my son but the only man I'd ever loved. So I left you to think things through.'

'Fi, I waited for you to come back.'

He had no idea how often she'd nearly returned, only she'd been afraid to face him and see the hurt she'd caused written in his eyes. And then there had been her guilt…

He continued, 'I rang your father daily, asking if you were with him, but he always fobbed me off by saying you wanted time to yourself. No one at the hospital knew where you'd gone, only that you'd resigned abruptly.'

'I did want time to myself. That's why I left in the first place.'

'I couldn't believe you'd disappear from my life so completely. At first I was angry with you, then as the days passed I blamed myself, felt I'd failed you in some way and that was why you'd left. As the years went by and I got really busy with this place I figured I'd only be raking up old wounds if I tracked you down. They were best left alone by then.' He stared at his hands, recalling the anguish of those weeks. 'Where did you go when you left me?'

'I got an apartment on Auckland's Viaduct, overlooking the harbour. It should've been soothing and healing; instead I found everything to be cold and sterile.' She shivered. 'I'd lost the two most important people in the whole wide world. Almost overnight my reason for living had gone. Looking back, I wonder if I didn't go a little bit crazy… I took my plane and flew the length and breadth of the country, trying to break every private pilot record standing. But it didn't dull the pain one iota. So I took up aerobatics. I became careless of myself. Unfortunately, or thankfully,

I'm a natural when it comes to flying. No matter how hard I pushed all the boundaries I couldn't get it wrong enough to write myself off.'

Once more Tom hooked her up in his arms and drew her close, cuddled her. 'You idiot,' he muttered, but understanding laced his voice.

'Yep. A total fool. Then one day it all caught up with me.' She snapped her fingers. 'Just like that. I fell apart. Completely. I cried for six months. I lost so much weight my father had me hospitalised and fed intravenously. But in the long run it worked out for the best.'

'How's that?'

'One day the television in my hospital room was tuned to the Discovery channel, and I didn't have the energy to get out of bed to find the remote and change the channel. One of the nurses used to deliberately leave the remote out of reach so I'd have to make an effort. Her ploy didn't work very often. So this day I lay watching how the poverty-stricken women of the Sudan coped with raising their children in appalling conditions. I'd always known about third world countries. Who didn't? But I'd never really taken it in other than on a superficial level. That day I did. My wealthy, self-indulgent lifestyle shamed me. That programme changed my life, and gave me a focus for getting out of hospital.'

'So you went to London?'

'I still hadn't sorted out my feelings about what had happened to us, so I thought I needed to put as much space as possible between you and me. I couldn't get much further away than England and still be able to finish my training. That's where I heard about Global Health. The rest, as they say, is history. My history, anyway.'

'It's an impressive one.'

'I know. It's nothing like what you'd have expected of me. I surprised myself sometimes. There were days working for Global Health when the temperatures were in the forties, and exasperating equipment malfunctions were undermining our hard work, and I'd look around, wondering what I was doing. But if someone had come up to me with a ticket out, even at the worst times I'd never have taken it. I really believed in what I was doing. It has to have been the most rewarding work I've ever done.'

Tom shook his head and smiled back. 'It does seem a little odd to imagine you in such extreme conditions. I admire you. I'm sure you're downplaying the hard times.'

'Surprised?' She raised an eyebrow. She hadn't been known for her lack of forthrightness about herself. It just went to show that people sometimes could change. She'd had enough hard knocks to instigate a mammoth makeover.

The cold air sent a shiver through her body. Not so long ago they'd been kissing and her blood had been boiling. Tightening the quilt around her, she snuggled closer to Tom. Again she thought she really shouldn't be here in Tom's bedroom, lying on his bed with him. Their relationship wasn't like that now. Her smile faded as sadness enveloped her.

Tom must have sensed her change of mood. Or he'd realised the same thing at the same time as she had. They'd always had an uncanny ability to read each other's minds. Whatever the reason, he now sat up straighter and swung his legs over the edge of the bed, rested his forearms on his thighs.

'How often have you been home since you left for London?'

His question startled her. 'This is the first time.'

His eyes widened. 'Really?'

'I may have found a focus for my life but I'd

still lost Liam and you. I didn't feel I belonged here any more.'

'What about your father?'

'It was time to do what was right for me, not something designed to get Dad's attention.'

'That must have been interesting,' Tom drawled. 'How'd he take that?'

'He refused to believe I'd waste my training on "the poor people of the world". Dad's words, not mine. When he couldn't change my mind about who I worked for, he tried a different tack. You wouldn't believe the offers I received for partnerships.'

Tom frowned. 'Wouldn't I?'

'Okay, maybe you would. But once the message clanged home that I wasn't taking up any of those offers he turned off the money supply into my bank account. Figured that would have me racing back so fast I'd have passed a meteor on the way.'

'You didn't?'

She had to chuckle at the amusement in Tom's voice. 'I knew you'd have a problem believing that one.'

Until then her father had always given her a very substantial allowance. He was a wealthy man, and in his book wealthy men provided well for their families.

She added, 'After that Dad changed. It's as though he respects me for who I am now, not who he wanted me to be. I'm still a little cautious around him, but we're getting on a lot better these days.'

'Which is all you ever wanted from him in the first place.'

I like this Fiona, Tom thought as he absorbed yet another change in her. She was intriguing him with her new attitude to life.

These past days of working together, sharing his cottage, had given him the feeling of how it had used to be when he and Fi were married. Cosy, even fun. He liked coming home at the end of a busy day to find Fiona already there, pottering around in the kitchen. It wasn't the meals she prepared, it was the company. In particular *her* company.

Careful, he warned himself. *Remember you swore that you'd never, ever, let Fiona near your heart again. No matter what.*

True, but she *is* different, his heart argued.

Which is good, but I once loved the old Fiona.

Look what happened there. I'm too vulnerable to the depth of love we shared. It hurts too much when it goes wrong, and there are no guarantees it won't happen again.

Coward. His heart had the last word.

CHAPTER EIGHT

'DID you ever forgive me for Liam's death?' Fiona whispered.

'What?' Tom's jaw dropped as shock slammed into him. Fiona had blamed *herself* for Liam's death? No way! 'You can't have blamed yourself for what happened. What could you have done to save him? It was cot death, for pity's sake. No one can prevent that. It creeps in and steals life,' Tom choked. His heart pounded painfully against his ribs.

'I always blamed myself. Surely you knew that?' Her eyes were huge in her pale face. 'What if I hadn't put him on his right side, knowing that he tended to roll over? Or what if I'd sat with him a little bit longer that night? He'd been colicky earlier in the evening. Had I missed him crying out in his sleep? Anything—everything—that could possibly have happened, even an uneven breath, I wish I'd been in Liam's bedroom to know about it.'

'If only I'd known you felt like that.' He'd have tried to save her a whole heap of anguish. But he hadn't known—because he hadn't listened. He had let her down, big-time. Would she ever forgive *him*? Maybe if he explained his feelings of helplessness back then, how he'd been trying to save her some grief.

Tom stood up and lifted Fiona into the bed and climbed in beside her, tugging the bedcovers over them. He lay down along her back, hooked am arm over her waist and held her against him. He tried to warm her as she shook continuously.

'Listen to me, Fi. Never did I blame you. No one can predict Sudden Infant Death Syndrome. Nor can they save their baby from it. SIDS is widely written up by every expert under the sun. Not one of them purports that parents should sit with their babies every second of their lives. As hard as it is to accept, it happens.'

'I know,' she whispered. 'But I had to find a reason, and the only one I could come up with was that I'd done something wrong. I'm a doctor. I should've noticed something.'

'Put it like that and it's worse for me. I'm a paediatrician. Children, babies, are my specialty. I spent months reading every article I could get my hands on, but I'd always known the vagaries of the syndrome.' Which hadn't helped one iota.

'Did you ever? Blame yourself, I mean.'

'Of course I did—for a damned long time. But eventually I saw reason. I've seen enough distraught parents of babies who've died of SIDS to know that they're the first to blame themselves, and that they're invariably wrong. They couldn't have prevented it and neither could we. Doctors aren't immune to these things.'

'Thank you. I'm glad I came here this week, even if I've disturbed you. This is something we needed to share.' Her voice sounded clogged with tears.

He held her tight for a moment, remembering how they'd used to lie like this to go to sleep every night. And how invariably Fiona would fall asleep and, as she relaxed, start poking him with her elbow, tapping him with her heels. Even in sleep she'd been restless. He nibbled his bottom lip. He'd loved those moments with her. He'd missed her so much when she'd gone away. Not just for the big things, but the little things that were special between couples.

Tom flipped onto his back, shuffled sideways, putting a space between them. They were getting way too cosy. Lying in his bed, holding her in his arms was dangerous, no matter that they were fully clothed. The situation fogged his mind, blanked out reality. Which was what? That they were no longer a couple. That he still cared for her, but there could be no future for them together. Their marriage had failed first time round. What could possibly make it work if they tried again?

Did he want to try? Was he afraid to try? Yes. And yes.

Fiona rolled the other way and sat up to lean back against the pillows. Had she felt the same danger?

'Did you really never wonder where I'd gone? Try to follow me?'

'At first I kept thinking you'd be back, that I had to give you the space you so obviously wanted. But as time went on and you didn't return I began to accept you didn't love me any more.' He'd waited endlessly, stubbornly refusing to go after her, wrongly thinking she had to make the first move.

'I'm here now.' She paused, then, 'I did love you when I left. But I had to go. We weren't working. I couldn't deal with anything any more.'

She *had* loved him—as in the past. His lungs seemed to stop functioning; air clogged his chest. So there really was no hope of rekindling their marriage. *Well, idiot, haven't you always known that? Admit it, all those years you waited for her to come back you knew deep down she didn't love you any more. What happened to keeping Fi at arm's length this week? See, you're calling her Fi again. Talk about setting yourself up for the long drop.*

Anyway, he should be relieved. He'd never wanted to get as deeply involved with a woman again as he had been with Fiona. He'd given his heart once. To do it twice and have it rejected would be foolish—especially if that second time was to the same woman.

Fiona was still talking, and he wanted to ignore her, but he heard her loud and clear.

'I know I was spoilt, impetuous and fiery, and we had some tempestuous times, but we were great together, you and I. Great enough to survive what happened to Liam if only we'd known how. I really believe that. Talk to me, Tom.'

Sure thing. Spill his guts and then get on with his life.

Her fingers dug into her palms as she willed

him to answer. But when he did, he thought he'd never seen anyone looking so desolate. But he had to stop this conversation in its tracks. It wasn't doing either of them any good. He felt as though he was standing on the edge of a precipice, totally unsure where he was going.

'It's too late for us, Fiona. I have other responsibilities now.' His heart ached. He'd missed her in his life so much. Damn it. He wanted to grab her up and hold her for ever. But he wouldn't.

Loud knocking, followed by the front door being thrown back against the wall, had his head jerking round.

'Tom, are you here? There's been an accident down by the bridge and you're needed.' Stella's voice echoed through the cottage as she advanced down the hall. He saw her pass the bedroom door, heard her heavy steps stop, backtrack to the bedroom.

'Tom? I'm sorry. I should've stayed outside knocking, but it's urgent.'

Tom crawled out from under the bedcovers, glad of the interruption. 'What's this about an accident?'

'A car skidded on ice at the approach to the one-way bridge and slammed into the bank.

Pierce says the snow-laden bank took some of the impact, but to him the injuries look serious. Robert's already there, but he needs a hand.'

'How many people are injured? And where are my keys?' Tom searched through his pockets.

'On the top of the fridge.' Fiona brushed past Stella, still standing in the doorway. 'I'll get them. I'm coming with you.'

'Two couples. They're here for the golf tournament. According to Pierce, alcohol's involved. And, worse, the road is treacherous between here and the highway to Christchurch. He doesn't think you'll get an ambulance through tonight.'

Tom followed Fiona into the kitchen, with Stella right on his heels. He caught the keys Fiona tossed to him and swiped up his jacket.

'Pierce is the local cop, and Robert's our GP,' he explained to Fiona on their way to his vehicle. 'We'll be busy if the injuries are serious, and if the road's as bad as Pierce says we'll have to bring the victims back here.'

Fiona grimaced. 'The injured people can be thankful you've got such a well-equipped theatre. Have we got kits to take to the scene?'

'Liz is getting two ready,' Stella answered.

'Hop in, Fiona,' Tom called to her. 'Stella, can

you get Theatre ready in case we have to perform surgery? Can you also phone Kerry and warn her we might need her?'

'Of course. Have you got your cell phone so you can let us know what's happening?'

'I'll get Pierce to phone through.'

A figure loomed up through the murky night air. 'Here you go, Tom. Two bags full of everything I could think of.'

'Thanks, Liz. Can you give Stella a hand, and stay on in case you're needed later?'

As Liz answered in the affirmative Tom already had the engine revving, and Fiona slammed her door shut. She shivered, and said, 'I wouldn't have thought this town was big enough to have its own GP.'

'Robert Greison is semi-retired. His wife died of cancer two years ago, leaving him with two teenaged boys. He decided to bring them here, where he could practise part time and be with the lads at the weekends and school holidays. They go to boarding school in Christchurch during the week.'

Tom drove carefully on the treacherous road, and a few minutes later lights beckoned through the falling snow.

Fiona pointed. 'Looks like that's it.'

Parking where directed, Tom shoved his door open and saw Fiona flinch as the bitterly cold air snatched at her. But she braced herself and gingerly stepped down onto the slippery roadside. After grabbing the kitbags from the back seat, she followed him to the wrecked car, lying on its side in a ditch. A tow truck had backed up close to the front of the vehicle, its strong searchlights lighting up the area brighter than day. Two people—presumably men, though it was hard to tell with their thick jackets and woollen hats—were squatting down beside someone lying on a stretcher.

Screams rent the air spasmodically. The hairs rose on the back of Tom's neck as he hurried towards the wreck, Fiona at his side. Someone needed them. He and Fiona were here to help. That, at least, felt good.

'Hey, Tom!' A deep male voice boomed out from beside the car and one of the figures rose from next to the inert body. 'Over here.'

Tom took Fiona's elbow and led her across to introduce her to Robert and Pierce. 'Thought an extra medic wouldn't go astray.'

Robert eyed Fiona up and down. 'Even better.

You're slim and might be able to squeeze inside beside the guy jammed under the dashboard. He's unconscious. I've managed to reach in and establish there's a pulse. A lot of blood too, but I'm not sure where from. It's tricky getting to him with the car tipped over like it is.'

'Sure—anything you want. Do we have a name?' Fiona asked.

'Dave Fergusson, according to the women passengers.'

As Fiona snapped on latex gloves Tom felt a hitch around his heart. He didn't want her putting herself in any danger by climbing into that scrunched vehicle. Jagged metal could tear clothing and skin in an instant. A sudden question came to him. 'What about airbags?'

'Deactivated,' a fireman replied.

'You don't have to do this,' he murmured to Fiona. 'That mangled wreck will be full of hazards. And it doesn't look terribly steady, lying on its side.'

'I'll be fine, and as Robert pointed out no one else will fit through that narrow gap that used to be a window.'

Tom knew she was right, but that only made him want to try harder to dissuade her from her mission—and yet he understood she'd agreed to go in because a man needed her doctoring skills. Fiona would never let him down. 'You'd better watch out for pieces of metal. You'll slice yourself if you're not careful.'

She gave him a smile and nudged him. 'Tom, just help me up and stop worrying. I don't think I can squeeze in without a bit of a shove from behind.'

'You haven't grown any over the years, have you?' He tried to lighten the panic in his heart and bent so she could stand on his thigh, his hands holding her around her waist until she was steady. Even as he let her go he wanted to snatch her back against him, keep her safe. So much for keeping her at arm's length.

Placing her feet carefully around her patient, she bent down awkwardly. 'Can someone get me a torch?'

A low, keening moan filled the air as Tom saw Fiona carefully feel the man's head, talking softly, reassuringly, all the time.

'Dave, I'm a doctor. You've been in an accident. Can you hear me?'

The man didn't answer.

'Here's the torch. Tell me what you find as you

go, then I'll know what equipment to get you.' Tom peered into the wreck, frustrated at having to wait outside.

The full horror of the scene was apparent in the yellow beam. Fiona's patient stared sightlessly, his face streaked with blood. Blood coated everything. If it was all his, the man had lost too much.

Inside the vehicle, Fiona talked as she worked with her patient. 'I'm starting with his ribs, hoping we're not dealing with a flail chest. As far as I can tell the ribs have not been pushed into the chest cavity.'

'One thing in his favour, then. How about his airways?'

'Clear, and his breathing's laboured but regular.'

'Good.' Would she hurry up and get out of there?

'Can you pass me a sphygmomanometer?'

The blood pressure reading was important; a low one could indicate a continuing bleed somewhere.

'Is it possible for you to reach his arm and hold it still?' Fiona asked.

Tom pushed his shoulders through the narrow

gap as far as he could until the squashed window frame prevented further movement. 'I've got a cervical collar too. Damned if I know where Liz found it, but I'm grateful to her.'

He held the patient's arm while Fiona inserted an intravenous line for much needed morphine and fluids. Then she took the blood pressure reading.

'BP's too low,' she said.

Tom watched as Fiona gently probed her patient's abdomen. Then her hands moved down his body until Tom heard a grunt of satisfaction. 'Torn artery at the top of his leg.'

Stretching out, Tom helped apply the pressure needed to slow and gradually halt the bleeding.

Fiona said softly, 'He's also got a huge swelling above the left eye, so possibly there are cranial injuries. We need to fit the neck collar, and that's not going to be easy. He's caught between the gearstick and the seat, and his body's twisted at an angle so his lower back's stuck under the front of the car.'

As they struggled with the collar one of the tow truck drivers came up beside Tom. 'We're ready to lift the engine block back so you can get your man out of there. Just give us the nod.'

Tom raised an eyebrow at Fiona. 'What do you think? Is he ready?'

'There's nothing more I can do for him here, and the sooner we have him out the sooner he gets to hospital.'

'Fi, come out of there. You're only giving them something else to worry about if you're in the car too.' Did he have to beg her? 'I want you out.'

She climbed gingerly back through the narrow window space. He tugged her away, thankful to have her out of the vehicle unscathed as the tow truck swung its enormous steel hook over the bonnet.

'Have you heard how the guy on the ground is?' Fiona asked as she sheltered in front of him from the cold breeze.

Just then Robert appeared beside them and answered Fiona's question. 'Broken femur, suspected punctured lung, and possibly a ruptured spleen. He took a hard landing on the road, but he could've been a lot worse off. We've put him in the back of my vehicle. Once we've got your man out, we'll head back to the hospital.'

'I thought there were four people in the car.' Tom peered around, suddenly aware of raised voices coming from inside the police four-wheel drive vehicle.

'Two women were in the back seat and they fared a lot better than their husbands. But they're rather intoxicated and argumentative. Pierce has got his hands full with them as he tries to find out what happened. He's also keeping them out of the way while we deal with their husbands.'

'No injuries at all?' He sympathised with Pierce. Dealing with inebriated people in these situations was always like walking on ice.

'One of them needs her chin stitched. It's a very long, jagged gash.'

Tom sighed. 'Then she can be thankful we've got a plastic surgeon in town.'

'I'll take a look once we've sorted these other two out.' Fiona stamped her feet and hugged her upper body.

'Your teeth are clacking.' Tom draped an arm around her shoulders and tucked her neatly under his arm in an attempt to give her some warmth from his body. A purely altruistic gesture, of course.

'Clacking? I'm not a castanet.'

'Are too.' His need to protect her swelled like a balloon filling with air.

A horrendous sound of screeching metal tore through the air as the engine block was lifted away from the seriously injured man. Immediately Fiona left Tom's side to supervise the man's removal. In no time at all they were on the road, heading for Tom's hospital and the operating theatre.

And Tom tried to remind himself why he shouldn't want Fiona working alongside him at his hospital. It wasn't easy.

'What a night.' Fiona stretched her back.

'Guess you're not used to this where you've been.' Stella handed Fiona suture thread to stitch Dave Fergusson's torn artery.

'Not a lot of car accidents in Pakistani villages.' Fiona concentrated on their patient. With the artery repaired she turned to the head wound, which appeared to be superficial. Enough to knock the man unconscious and give him concussion, but otherwise it appeared he'd escaped serious head injuries. To be on the safe side, Fiona ordered a cranial X-ray as well as X-rays of his chest.

While an orderly wheeled her patient to the radiology room she crossed over to help Tom and

Robert. Tom glanced up at her, and grimaced. 'Not quite what you were expecting when you signed on for the week, was it?'

'It's all medicine to me. It's what I do, who I am.'

'Keep that up and I'll be offering you a permanent position here. We can agree that we work well together in any medical situation.' Tom winked, then stilled, as though it had only then occurred to him what he'd offered.

Fiona felt warmth trickle through her at the idea he wanted her around. Of course Tom probably now regretted opening his mouth. But they *had* worked well together throughout the night. If they could do this, why couldn't they put their differences behind them?

'Fiona?' Robert was talking to her. 'We're missing the top knuckle of a thumb here. Want to work some of your plastic surgery magic on the guy?'

Grateful for the distraction, she set to work, concentrating hard. But it was Tom who handed her equipment as she requested it, almost before she'd asked. He anticipated all her moves, as if they were a partnership. Warmth seeped through her again, and she held it around her like a shawl.

'What time is it?' Fiona laid the suture thread down for the last time and straightened her aching back.

'Three-fifty-five,' Liz called across the room. 'It's been a long night, hasn't it?'

Tom agreed. 'Thank goodness for those Christchurch specialists.'

Some of the surgery required on the two men had been out of the scope of a paediatrician, a GP and a plastic surgeon. But with the help of specialists at the other end of the phone they had succeeded in repairing injuries, removing organs and keeping both men alive.

'I've requested the medic helicopter ASAP,' Tom told everyone over hot coffee and plates of bacon and eggs, cooked by one of the hospital's cooks who'd come in early especially. 'But at the moment Hanmer Springs is completely blocked off by the storm that's apparently been battering us most of the night.'

'Wouldn't know a thing, locked up in here,' Liz noted.

'What chance has the pilot got of getting through if this storm has headed on down through Canterbury?' Fiona knew that storms could stall over areas, but she didn't know the normal drift of a storm in the vicinity of these particular ranges.

'The dispatch officer seemed fairly confident that we'd be seeing the helicopter some time around ten this morning.' Tom yawned into his mug. 'In the meantime I'll brief the staff and give all of you the morning off.'

Fiona didn't feel tired. Rather, exhilaration bubbled through her veins. They'd all worked together to save the lives of two men. They'd also patched up the minor injuries the two women had suffered. This was what she'd trained for, even if her specialty wasn't emergency medicine. To help people. And working with Tom had been a bonus. Oh, yes, she was buzzing. She didn't need to take the morning off to recuperate. Instead she felt ready for anything.

'You can't be thinking of postponing this morning's schedule, surely?' she queried Tom.

'Absolutely. We'll start operating at eleven instead of eight. That should give everyone a few hours' sleep.' Tom rolled his eyes at her. 'Including you. I can see you're firing on all cylinders now, but once that huge stack of food you're pouring down your throat hits your stomach you're going to slow down. Throw in a hot shower, and you'll be toast.'

'Sounds wonderful.' A hot shower. Delicious. That was something they didn't often get after a long, difficult shift out in the villages she'd been working in.

The thought of that scorching water pummelling her back had her in raptures. She sighed and stretched out on the chair, her legs pushing under the table, her arms crossed behind her head. Closing her eyes, she imagined standing under the steaming jets, imagined Tom sharing it with her as he'd often used to. Her skin heated up in anticipation and she opened her eyes to find Tom gazing at her, the tip of his tongue wetting his upper lip, his eyes smoky grey. The colour they went when he was aroused.

Excitement tingled over her skin. She knew Tom felt the pull between them. He wasn't immune to her after all. Joy zipped through her. She wanted to leap up and punch the air. There was a chance for them—hope. They could get back together, pick up the pieces, and start the loving all over again. Yes! The loving…the lovemaking. It had all started with a shower. The very first time. Tom was remembering that too. She saw it in his eyes. Even her skin had memories in all the sensitive places he had touched with his gentle fingers, with his hot, demanding tongue. And she wanted it again. Now. In Tom's shower back at the cottage.

She sat up straight. Made to stand. Smiled enticingly at Tom.

Stella loomed into view. 'I'll show Fiona where the staff bathrooms are. That way you can both get showered straight away. I'm sure Fiona wants to get some sleep as soon as possible.'

Confusion creased Tom's face, darkened his eyes. 'Not necessary. Fiona can use the cottage bathroom first. I've got a couple of things to attend to here before I call it quits.'

Fiona stumbled to the bench with her dirty plate and cup, dropped them into the sink and carelessly rinsed them, her heart slowing. The more time she spent with Tom, the harder it became to control her feelings for him.

That *had* been desire she'd seen in Tom's eyes a few minutes ago. She knew him only too well to be wrong.

Tom stamped down the corridor to the outside door leading out into the expansive grounds. He needed air, and plenty of it.

Once again he'd been sidetracked by Fiona. She had a knack of making him feel as though he was coming alive for the very first time in years. Her very presence made him understand he had a lot to live for. Back there in the cafeteria he'd been in that shower with her. He'd wanted to wash her back, her arms, those legs he'd always got so turned on over. Damn it. He had to stop this.

Fiona had been turned on, he'd swear. Her eyes had widened in that misty kind of way they had. Her breasts had pushed against the thick layers of clothing she wore, reminding him of their warm fullness and satin smoothness in his larger, rougher hands.

The banging of the door behind him echoed in the freezing air. The snow had stopped; the wind had died down. In the dark, the white blanket lying over the lawns was eerie wherever lights from inside shone through the windows. He loved this place. Even in extreme weather conditions it was beautiful. Right now, when the storm had passed and everything lay quiet and still, this was when he loved it the most.

But Fiona had him thinking about other things. She'd become the wild card in his carefully put-together life. And he didn't know how to deal with this.

He knew what he wanted to do. He ached to race back to his cottage, throw open the shower door and step in with her. He'd slide his arms around under her breasts. He'd take the soap from her hand and lather those soft mounds. Her nipples would grow taut and she'd arch her back, leaning against him, her bottom sliding against his erection.

He'd turn her around, his mouth finding hers so he could kiss her until she couldn't control herself. That was when she'd hook her legs up around his waist, and take him into her. And they'd be completely together again.

That was how he wanted to deal with the turbulent emotions she had set off inside him. But he wasn't going to do any of that. Making love would not solve a thing. Since working with Fiona to release Dave Fergusson from that crushed wreck he found he couldn't still the sensation that he was missing some point. He'd hated it when she'd put herself at risk. The fear was an old feeling—one he'd known whenever she flew her plane. She'd told him she didn't take risks any more, and compared to what she used to do climbing into that wreck had been fairly tame. She'd been careful of herself and her patient. It was the same care she'd taken with all her patients this week.

He liked this new Fiona. His feelings weren't just about love and lust, but about friendship and caring. Scary stuff. He wasn't ready for anything like this.

Which was why he'd go back into the hospital and use the bathroom put aside for medical staff. A cold shower might do the trick. At least his heart should be safe there for a short while.

CHAPTER NINE

'HEY, Sophie, how're you doing?' Fiona sat on the end of the girl's bed and stifled a yawn. Tom had been right. Exhaustion had hit her after the early breakfast, and the three hours' sleep she'd managed hadn't been nearly enough.

Sophie lowered the teen magazine she'd been flicking through in a desultory fashion. 'I'm bored. Dad's gone to the shops to get me some more magazines, but I'm sick of reading.'

'How about getting up and going to see the other kids stuck in bed? Some of the little ones are getting fidgety too, and they would love to see someone new.'

'I'd scare them with this face.'

'Sophie! Shame on you. You're beautiful, remember?' Fiona struggled to keep the sorrow out of her voice. It wouldn't help Sophie to know that her surgeon felt sad for her. 'Every one of these kids has got scars they're dealing with. You're not alone. They need their confidence boosted, just like you, and I happen to think you're the right person to do that.'

'One scarred person to another, you mean?'

'Exactly.' Fiona refused to let Sophie's self-pity rule her. 'You understand what these kids are feeling. And the big thing is you're not much older than most of them, so they will relate to you far more than they can to me.'

'What would I say to them?' Sophie bit her fingernail.

'You don't have to say anything unless they specifically ask you a question, and then it's more likely to be about you than them. Read to them, or play a game of cards.'

'That's all?' There was a glimmer of hope in the girl's eyes.

Fiona knew Sophie felt nervous about approaching strangers, even those younger than herself. 'Come on—out of bed. We're going visiting.'

'Can't I get dressed? I look silly walking around in my bathrobe.'

A delaying tactic. 'All your new friends are in their pyjamas. Anyway, I'm due in surgery in the next twenty minutes and haven't got time to wait while you get all glammed up.'

Sophie suddenly grinned at her. 'I'm young. It doesn't take that long.'

'As in I'm not so young, and need a concrete mixer for the amount of make-up I require? Brat.' Fiona knuckled her affectionately on the arm.

With Sophie well wrapped up in a deep green robe covered in dancing teddy bears they headed for the room next door, where two little girls sat in their beds giggling over something Fiona couldn't make any sense of.

'They're so cute,' Sophie whispered. 'What's wrong with them?'

The girls did look absolutely adorable. Fiona sighed, longing tugging at her. For a child. The longing quickly became a fierce pang, slamming through her. Until now she'd never believed that she'd ever want to be a mother again. Yet right now she'd give her heart to have another baby.

How could she think like this and not feel guilty about Liam? She should feel she was being unfaithful to her child by wanting another, but she didn't.

Her throat ached where her heart had lodged itself, pumping wildly. Her? Have another baby? Oh, yes. She breathed out slowly. But what if it died? She mightn't be strong enough to deal with that agony again. Then again, what if it grew up healthy and happy? Wouldn't that be wonderful?

'Hello? Fiona? Where have you gone?' Sophie waved her hand in front of Fiona's face.

'Sorry,' she gasped, and struggled to gather her thoughts. What had they been talking about?

'The little girls, what did they have done?'

Ahh. 'Nina had a skin graft on her thigh. She's the fair one. Jessie had some surgery on her ears. Now, come talk to them.' Fiona led Sophie forward to meet the now inquisitive youngsters.

By the time she left ten minutes later plenty of laughter could be heard coming from the room as a game of Happy Families got underway.

She poked her head around the next door to say hello to Shaun, but found his bed empty.

'He's down in the library with his mum,' Liz told her when she asked at the nurses' station. 'He's a lot happier today, now that his sore throat is responding to those different antibiotics you prescribed.'

'Good. How's his appetite? Any improvement?'

'Not really, but Tom had some more bloods drawn and sent to Christchurch for testing. We haven't had any results back other than the positive EBV result for glandular fever.'

'What did Tom ask for?'

The man himself answered from the head nurse's room behind the station. 'I'm checking his hormones and liver functions.'

Crossing to the doorway, Fiona leaned against the framework. Tom looked exhausted. He couldn't have got much sleep this morning, wherever he'd gone. He hadn't been back to the cottage at all. A night on the bed in his consulting room?

'Shaun's LFTs will be abnormal since he has glandular fever.' She'd stick to being professional. 'Or do you think there's been an underlying liver dysfunction going on for a lot longer?'

'It crossed my mind. Although he's not jaundiced, it could be he's got a chronic condition. Hopefully we'll know later today, when the next batch of results comes through. The lab's running behind with those particular tests. I'd have expected them by now.'

Liz spoke over Fiona's shoulder. 'I'll ring and ask about them.'

'Thanks.' Tom tossed his pen aside and shoved his chair back. 'Guess it's time for surgery again.

There's also another trip to the pools this evening, if you're interested.'

'I'll be there.' The water would warm her again.

Walking down the stairs leading to the operating theatre, Fiona still felt unsettled, and she blamed that on her sudden desire for a baby. Having Tom striding alongside her didn't help. She focused on Shaun instead. 'I hope we can solve Shaun's problem soon. The sooner he's getting the right treatment the better.'

Tom agreed. 'I think he'll go ahead in leaps and bounds once we've sorted the situation.'

She looked up at him. His attitude was completely professional this morning. Keeping his distance, she presumed. Come to think of it, he'd been that way since they were called to the accident. And she'd thought they might be getting closer. There was that mind-blowing kiss… At the moment his lips were straight, tight, as if he was holding something in, but she vividly recalled how they'd felt against hers last night. Soft and strong. Earthy and male. A kiss shouldn't hold such power, have such impact, but Tom's certainly did. It had been in her dreams that morning.

The second blinding realisation of the day slammed her.

She loved Tom. Still loved him. And if she was going to have another baby this was the only man she'd ever consider having one with.

There it was. As clear as an autumn sky. Her stomach clenched, squeezed, made her catch her breath. How could she not have known her own feelings? Love was a huge emotion. She should have been aware of it, should have felt it in her bones, in the very air she breathed.

What now? She loved this wonderful, caring man, and on Saturday she'd have to walk away from him. Again. She couldn't do it.

She had to do it. He'd made it abundantly clear he might care for her, but he didn't love her.

So she'd have to make the most of the few days she had left with him. Her shoulders drooped as her stomach cramped. No, she'd have to settle for professional conversations, working together in Theatre, and snatched dinners in the cottage before he dashed back to the hospital.

What did he do over here late at night? There would be a lot of administrative work in running this place, and Tom probably didn't get time during the day to look at it, what with patients and staff demanding his attention every minute of every hour. If only she could stay on and help him. Another truth hit home. She'd love nothing more than living and working here beside Tom, helping keep the hospital going.

Pain jagged her. There wasn't a place for her in the life he'd carved out. He only needed a plastic surgeon a few weeks of the year, and he didn't seem to want a wife at all.

'You've gone quiet.' Tom turned to look down at her, his hands now jammed in his pockets. A raft of emotions raced across his face. Too many for her to read accurately, though she thought she recognised confusion, hope, and biggest of all worry. About what?

At least he couldn't read her mind. Then he'd really have something to worry about. How would he react if he knew how she felt? Better not go there.

'Did our accident patients get away to Christchurch Hospital?' she asked, in an attempt to bring her brain back into line and away from these disturbing thoughts.

'Yes. The ambulances got here about an hour ago.'

As they pushed through the theatre doors,

dressed in their blue theatre gear, scrubbed and ready to go, Kerry looked up and waved. 'Hi, you two. Thought we'd have to start without you.'

'Are we late?' both Fiona and Tom asked in unison, then smiled at each other.

Fiona concentrated hard throughout the four operations she performed that afternoon. But between patients, as she scrubbed up and waited for the next child, her mind kept returning to Tom and her love for him. At the end of the day she was still none the wiser about what to do about it. Except put it back where it had laid dormant for years.

The noise level in their section of the main pool was horrendous, with Fiona adding her share of yells to the mix. Everyone had joined in a game of water bull rush, with the kids winning hands down.

'I'd rather be sitting in front of a roaring fire with a glass of red wine in my hand,' one mother moaned good-naturedly as she ducked aside from two charging boys and got dunked by another for her efforts.

Fiona pushed sopping hair out of her eyes, agreeing. 'You forgot the Brie and crackers.'

'Pathetic, the pair of you,' Tom quipped behind her. 'What could be better than joining in with these guys, having fun?'

'I think we just answered that one.' Pleased that Tom had joined them, Fiona nearly missed seeing two children suddenly dive, aiming directly for her legs. As she lunged sideways, she added, 'In the meantime, I'm not letting these two stop me getting to the other end and claiming my point.'

Strong arms caught her around the waist and Tom said, 'But I am. I'm on their side.'

Fiona wriggled in his hold. 'You can't do that. You're an adult; you've got to play for our side.' How was she supposed to remain aloof when he did this?

Tom held her easily. 'Caught Doc Fiona!' he yelled to one of the girls.

Even in the tepid water Fiona was very aware of the heat from Tom's hands. Heat that had a lot to do with her body's reaction to the man she still wanted to call her husband. She held herself stiff, stopped wriggling.

Tom's eyebrows rose. 'Give in?'

'Never.' Her toes reached for the bottom of the pool, found Tom's shins. Even that small contact sent her blood zinging. Which was such an over-the-top reaction that she blushed. Hopefully he wouldn't notice in the rising steam.

But when she lifted her face to peer at him she knew he understood exactly how she felt. His hands were slowly bringing her closer to his body, her thighs against his, her hands gripping his forearms. It felt incredibly right to be here in Tom's arms. He was the only man who'd ever made her feel so secure and so sexy all in one hit. With Tom she'd always felt alive. That was how she felt right now. Her body had begun awakening from a deep sleep. It had been so, so long since she'd felt anything as exciting as this. Tendrils of desire unfurled at the pit of her stomach.

'Fi.' It was almost a gasp.

Such a little word, his name for her, but so full of meaning, so coloured with what had been between them before, so laden with what might be now if only they could find the way back to each other.

You can't afford to get too close. Not even once. It will hurt when it's over and you've gone away.

The zinging stopped. Her blood became sluggish, her heart heavy. Too heavy. She'd waited too long, had come back too late. Tom had moved on.

She gave his arms a light squeeze and slid away. His hands let go their hold instantly, his gaze perplexed. Pushing through the water, she made for the end of the pool and hauled herself out. It was too dangerous for her peace of mind to stay in the pool any longer. She'd change into dry clothes and stay on the sidelines as the duty doctor. That way there'd be less damage done to her heart.

On the bus returning to the hospital, she caught Tom's brooding gaze on her. His intensity unnerved her.

When the bus stopped outside the front door Tom waited for her to disembark. 'I hear there's another lion game tonight. Need a lion?' His tone was tentative. 'Only thing is, if I'm needed can we do it sooner rather than later? I've got to go out at seven.'

Rubbing her forehead with the heel of her hand, she grimaced. 'With the way today's shaped up I'd totally forgotten about the game. Will the kids be ready now? What about their dinner?'

'The little ones will have eaten, and will be

scrubbed and in their pyjamas ready for story-time and bed.'

'Then I guess now's as good a time as any.' She turned to head to the children's lounge. With noisy kids milling around, even walking beside Tom and talking about normal things was difficult. All she wanted was to slide her arms around his upper body and hug him to her.

'I'll see you there. I need to check my messages first.' Tom's voice sounded neutral as he stepped back, but she sensed an underlying current of emotion in the tightening of his shoulders, the way he'd suddenly shoved his hands into his pockets. As though he was trying too hard to look casual and relaxed. He forgot—she did know him very well.

Actually, she'd also forgotten he knew *her* very well. So he fully understood her feelings, her burning desire for him. She might as well be standing there naked for all her efforts to hide her true feelings from him. If anyone on this earth understood her, Tom did.

Tom shoved the pad aside and stretched out in his chair. 'Thanks for covering those weeks, Kerry. I know it's never easy for you to do extra hours.'

'You can pay me in gold bullion if you like.' Kerry grinned.

'I'll get some out of my security box next time I go to the bank.'

'I'd better get home. The girls will have Craig wound around their little fingers well and truly by now.'

Tom grinned. 'Yeah, and he'll be loving every minute of it.' His goddaughters were adorable bundles of mischief. A sense of missing out caught him, made him wistful for what might have been if only he and Fiona had been able to work things out between them. Look how well she'd slotted in here. So well he wondered how he'd manage when she left again.

Kerry pushed out of her chair. Tom thought she looked exhausted. It must be draining, holding down a demanding job and raising two three-year-olds. He had an idea.

'Why don't you and Craig book a weekend somewhere warm and romantic, and I'll look after the twins?' That was something he could easily do, and he'd enjoy spending time with his goddaughters. They were the closest he had to family. A lump closed his throat. Family. He shivered. The room had gone cold.

'We might take you up on that.'

'I mean it.' Tom reached for his heavy ski jacket. 'Think I'll go outside for a walk.'

'You're going to wear a track around the hospital soon. I've seen you out there a lot this week.'

'Just like to get some fresh air.'

'Yeah, right.' Kerry got in the last word.

The air had icicles in it. Tom shivered, shoved his hands into the pockets of his jacket, his mind already turning to Fiona. As if he'd ever actually stopped thinking about her. Ever since that moment in the hot pools that afternoon he'd forgotten his determination to stay professional. When she'd leaned her body against his he'd gone hard in an instant. He'd seen the desire in her eyes, known that familiar sultry look meant she was hot for him. And he'd wanted her. Not just to make love to, but to hold and to cherish, for ever and a day.

'Hey, Doc, mind if I join you?' Jacob Clark appeared out of the gloom. 'I came out for a break from Sophie and all the medical stuff. Believe it or not, I hate being in hospitals. Never liked them.'

'A lot of people feel like that.' Usually because

of something unpleasant they or a loved one had experienced in the past. Tom wondered what had happened to Jacob, but didn't ask.

They walked along the meandering paths, talking about the latest rugby match, then about trout fishing.

'There's plenty of trout in the rivers around here,' Tom told the other man. 'You should give it a go while you're here, if you're keen.'

'Another time, maybe. This week's all about getting Sophie sorted.'

'I think she'll be very pleased with the results of her surgery once the swelling goes down.'

'It's all the other changes that I can't quite grasp. Don't get me wrong—I'm thrilled. It's just that I hadn't ever expected to see her laughing and talking non-stop again. Sophie's suddenly like she used to be.' There was wonder in Jacob's voice.

'She's happy.' Tom knew exactly who to thank for it. Fiona.

'Yes, that's it. It can't just be because she's had her operation, because at the moment her face is so swollen and bruised she looks worse than when she arrived. I'd have thought she'd be hiding under her pillows.'

There was a softening in Tom's muscles. 'Fiona happened, that's what. She won't let Sophie wallow in self-pity. Did you know that today she had Sophie entertaining two of the younger patients? Apparently that worked so well more little ones wanted Sophie to read to them.'

'My girl's confidence has been growing steadily since we came here. It's as though Fiona looks at the whole picture, not just the medical problem.'

Tom agreed. 'We need more people like her around here.'

He needed her around here. Never mind the hospital and the patients. He needed her.

Because he loved her! Had never stopped loving her.

Living without her had been hell. The innumerable nights he'd lain awake, willing her to come back. It had taken years to come to terms with his empty life, and immersing himself in hard work had been the only way to cope.

Jacob spoke through the darkening gloom. 'I'd better go back inside. I promised I'd have dinner with Sophie. Thanks for listening to me, Tom.'

Tom turned for another circuit of the grounds, all the while thinking about how well he and

Fiona worked together. Within the hospital community they had the same ethos. Each of them held the same need to care for those less fortunate, to provide the best medical care within their capabilities.

His toes stung when he kicked at the ice packed against the path. But it was nothing compared to the pain in his heart. Tipping his head back, he stared up at the black sky, begging the ache to stop, the torment of emotions to evaporate. He didn't *do* letting go of his emotions. That had been his strength—keeping everything close.

It hadn't worked with Fiona, though.

Dropping his head forward, he stumbled to a bench under an oak tree and sat, leaning with his head in his hands, his elbows on his knees. He ignored the cold wetness of the seat. What was a damp backside to a broken heart?

He watched the pictures flitting across his mind: scenes of their marriage; the good ones, the bad ones, even the ugly pieces. He felt the laughter and excitement, the anger and pain. All the integral parts of a relationship.

Finally his chattering teeth and the soul-deep cold brought him to his senses, and he found he'd finally let go his hold on all the agony that had been building since the day he'd lost Fiona, along with his beautiful son. For it might have been months later that Fiona had gone, but everything had begun falling apart the day of Liam's death.

He loved Fi.

That had not changed. Would she believe him if he were to tell her? Would she even want to know? She had wanted to make love with him today. That much had been very evident. But that wasn't the same as loving him.

He stood; his legs quivering, goosebumps raised on his skin. He needed to find Fiona. Not to tell her he loved her. That would be stirring up a wasps' nest. But it was time to really talk to her, to find out what she wanted to do next.

Did they have a future together? Did he want that? He thought he did.

Suddenly he couldn't wait another minute. He had to see her—explain himself. His feet slipped and skidded as he raced towards the cottage.

'Fi!' he called as he pushed open the front door.

Total silence greeted him. Her bedroom door was closed. His watch read nine-thirty. Had she gone to bed early? She'd been exhausted at the end of surgery.

His heart pounded so hard when he knocked on her door he thought his ribs would crack. What if she told him to get lost? He'd wasted too much time already. He needed this opportunity to explain himself.

The door opened a crack.

'Tom.'

Her flat voice frightened him.

'Can I come in?'

CHAPTER TEN

COMMON sense said no.

Fiona said yes.

Tom brushed past her as she held the door wider. He brought with him the cool night air. And a renewal of all the tension she'd felt in the pool earlier. One look at him and she was melting. Tugging the blanket tighter around her, she folded her arms across her breasts, trying to hold her desire at bay.

'Cold?' Tom asked, his eyes fixed on her face.

'A bit.' Which was blatantly untrue. Her cheeks glowed with heat. She scrutinised him back. 'Why are you here?'

'I needed to see you. To explain myself.'

A flicker of hope touched Fiona. Did this mean he was ready to talk about the issues surrounding them? Caution crept over her. What did she say next? She was afraid of getting it wrong, of turning him away because of another simple misunderstanding. Suddenly she was done with wanting to talk. The desire unfurling in her belly would not go back into hiding. It spread out, up and down, left and right. A throb began deep within her—a throb that would not be denied. To hell with talking. The time was past for that. They could talk until the sun came up, but they might not solve a darned thing.

She wanted Tom. *Now.* She'd deal with the consequences later.

But where and how to start? She was out of practice with everything when it came to men. Especially this one. All she knew was that she loved him and wanted to put things right—put things back the way they were before their marriage began disintegrating. They belonged together and she would fight for him.

She stepped closer, took his chilled hand in her warm ones. 'We had some good times, you and I.' There had been magic in their touches, in their love. She needed that magic back. Raising her arms to his solid chest, she lifted on to her tiptoes and placed a kiss below his chin, on the very sensitive spot that had always elicited a swift response.

'Yes, we did,' Tom whispered.

Shutting her eyes, she placed another butterfly kiss on his jaw. And heard a deep groan.

'Fi, I didn't come to—' Slowly, oh, so painfully slowly, his arms came up and wrapped her hard against him. His mouth found hers, his lips hot on her lips. His fingers dug into her hair, holding her head so he could kiss her thoroughly.

One taste of his mouth and she was lost. Completely. All week she'd been wanting words with this man. Now she couldn't think of a single one. The world began and ended here, held in that kiss. A kiss that deleted the intervening years since she'd left. A kiss that sent thrills of desire sweeping through her body like water on a drought-stricken field. Her hands gripped the front of his jacket. Her knees became boneless, and she fell against Tom. Tom. Her one love. Her real love.

She kissed him back with all the passion and sorrow and lost love of six years. This wasn't a kiss to entice him back to her; this was a kiss to give him everything she had to offer, to give him all of her.

He tasted as she remembered: hot and male.

His hands slid down her back, cupped her

bottom, hugged her closer against him so his arousal pressed into her stomach.

The blanket slid to the floor as her hips rocked against him, his indrawn breath encouraging her further. Her trembling fingers found the buttons of his shirt, fumbled with the openings. As the shirt fell open she dropped her mouth to his chest. The intoxicating taste of his skin sent every nerve-ending in her body into orbit.

Her hands fiddled with the zip of his trousers, the hard bulge beneath distracting her. She rubbed him through the fabric, impatient with the stubborn zip, needing to touch him, to claim him back. Hot, raging hunger grabbed her.

'I want your clothes off.' But she couldn't get the zip down.

She yanked his shirt out of the waistband. Ran her hands over his firm stomach, around his sides. Hot, silky skin against the palms of her hands. Heat zinged along her arms, down her body, signalling her feminine core to wake up. As her mouth followed the trail of her hand that heat built higher and higher, pummelling her with desire.

'Let me.' Tom's hands were between them, tugging at the zip, shoving his trousers down past his hips. When they fell around his ankles he quickly stepped out of them and kicked them aside.

Fiona's mouth dried at the sight of his long torso, dressed only in an open shirt. Beautiful. Sexy. 'I need you.'

Her hunger grew and the trembling in her fingers spread throughout her entire body. Biting down on her bottom lip, she raised her eyes to meet his wild gaze. Passion raged across his face, darkened his eyes. Passion for her.

Tom tugged her tee shirt over her head, exposing her breasts; then his hands were everywhere, touching her hips, her thighs, covering her breasts. Branding her. His thumbs rubbed her nipples until she nearly screamed with longing. When he reached for the moist place between her legs she could have wept with anticipation. For a brief moment she hesitated, viewing a rush of sweet, exquisite memories.

But reality far outweighed memories.

Her mouth continued kissing his body until she hadn't left any skin untouched, just as she'd wanted to do from the moment she'd first set eyes on him at the airstrip. Never in her wildest dreams had she imagined this feverish reunion. Never would she have believed it possible their passion would survive so completely after all their difficulties.

And when his hands grasped her bottom she almost leapt into his arms, succumbing to the pleasures he created. When he lifted her up she hooked her legs around his waist. Her need for him was so great she thought she'd blow apart if he didn't touch her sex soon. *Now.*

'Tom, please don't wait…' She puffed the words out.

He turned, backed her against the wall. 'As if I can.'

And then he was pushing into her. Hot bliss. Fiona's fingers dug into Tom's shoulders and her head tipped back as she took him deep inside. The rhythm built between them. Rapidly. Intensely. Explosively. Her body was no longer hers as she clung to the man she loved and felt him come inside her.

'So much for talking.' Tom's outstretched legs cut across the kitchen, where he sat by the table, dressed only in jeans. 'When you opened your bedroom door looking so tousled and beautiful I forgot everything I came about.'

Fiona looked at him and felt her heart slow. 'I hope you're not saying you regret making love.'

Disappointment tugged at her. Had she read too much into it because she loved him? Because she wanted him so much?

Tom looked shocked. 'How can you even think that?'

'I've been on a bit of an emotional rollercoaster this week. None of this has been easy for either of us.'

The afterglow of their lovemaking was rapidly fading from his face. 'I should've talked to you the day you arrived instead of putting it off. Truth? I should've talked to you years ago.' He paused.

She waited, holding her breath.

'There were times I nearly risked it, tried to tell you how I felt about Liam, my guilt, us. But I was so afraid that if I ever started I'd never stop. That I'd talk until I burned out and there'd be nothing left of me to go on with. That I'd have nothing to offer you.'

'You had heaps to give me. I know how much I needed you to open up, but there's more to you than being able to communicate with me. You've always been generous with your time, yourself, your intellect. Those are some of the reasons I loved you.'

His eyes widened briefly. His gaze was thoughtful, before he shook his head as though to rid it of something unpalatable. 'Don't, Fiona.'

Again that painful tightening of her stomach. He'd rebuffed her feelings in two words. *Don't, Fiona.* Yet they'd just been very passionate and intimate in the most loving way. Now confusion took over her brain, pushing aside the sublime happiness she'd been experiencing since they'd made love.

She continued talking as though he hadn't said that. 'You were a rock for me. But I can see that I expected too much of you. I shouldn't have pressed you to open up about what we were going through.'

'It was impossible for me to give you what you wanted. But I'm sorry I let you down so badly.'

'I think we let ourselves down more than anything.' She took a deep breath. 'I shouldn't have run away. If I'd stayed and waited until you felt able to communicate with me, able to share your grief, everything might have turned out differently. I'm so sorry.' She flicked her fingers across her thumb.

'We also might have gone on for a long time hurting each other, never finding our way back to each other, and therefore still destroying ourselves.'

'We'll never know.'

'We made a mess of things, didn't we?' Tom tipped his head to one side as he watched her. 'I guess our love wasn't as strong as we thought.'

A chill settled on her heart. So he *had* got over her. What else had she really expected? That he'd been waiting all these years for her to turn up and pick up where they'd left off? Was that what she'd wanted when she'd flown into Hanmer Springs the other day? Honestly? No. The most she'd hoped for was a reconciliation so they could become firm friends with a shared past.

Problem was it hadn't taken long for her to want more.

Tom got up and crossed to the bench, where he picked up the kettle. She wished he'd put his shirt on again. That bare chest created a distraction she didn't need right now. She tried to focus on his words and not his body.

He was saying, 'I thought I was being strong—for you *and* me. When Liam died I believed I had to hold it all together to help you through your grief. But you didn't want that. You wanted my soul bared, and I'd never done that for anyone before. I was afraid you'd find me lacking. That if you saw how torn up I'd become, how big a mess inside, you'd stop loving me.'

Her heart ached for him, and for what she hadn't seen at the time. She said, 'You kept avoiding me, staying at work so late that I'd be asleep when you got home. Then you'd be gone again when I woke in the morning. I thought you didn't want me any more.'

'Of course I wanted you, but I didn't know how to get through to you, how to handle you. I never seemed to be able to please you about anything. Staying at work became easier than going home. Then one day you were gone, and I'd lost my chance to fix things. Life became even worse. Hell, really. Liam followed me everywhere, haunting me with his big eyes, his gurgling laugh. You were right alongside him. Every time I went out the door to go to work I saw you—walking down the street with a baby in your arms, pushing a pram through the crowds on street corners, sitting in a café with Liam on your knees. I'd slam on the brakes, park the car haphazardly, and tear after you—only to find myself chasing a complete stranger. Finally I moved to Christchurch to get away from you both.'

'Did we follow you?'

'Occasionally you popped up, but as time went by it got easier. It helped that I was putting in such long hours that when I wasn't working I was sleeping. And as the plans for this place began taking shape my life sort of settled into a routine. Don't get me wrong. It was never the same. But it became liveable. I guess you can understand that.'

She sighed. 'Yes. You function, and occasionally you enjoy, even laugh, but it's like living with one limb missing.'

Very hard to cope.

Except she'd found that missing part again. Now she just had to work out how to reattach it.

'How did you manage?' Tom asked.

'I reached a point where I believed I'd used up my share of happiness, that there wouldn't be any more for me. I even thought it was punishment for my extravagant lifestyle. Now I'm not so sure. We've both spent the intervening years doing so much for other people, surely we're entitled to a little slice of happiness?' But how did Tom feel about her? Six years was a long time to keep love alive when there was so much distress and grief to deal with.

'Of course we are. Everyone is.' His aching sigh caught at her heartstrings. 'That's why we're clearing the air—so we can move on.'

That sounded very definitely like the slamming of a door. Fiona's intertwined fingers were white. Her teeth were grinding. Her thudding heart echoed in her ears, drowning out other sounds.

But he was asking her something. 'What's your next move? After here, I mean.'

'I'm still thinking about that. Initially I intended heading back overseas.' She hesitated a moment. 'But now—I don't know.'

'Why the change of mind?'

If she told him she wanted to settle here, in Hanmer Springs, would he be upset? Would he run a mile? She couldn't risk it. Not yet. 'I'm discovering I'm happy to be back in New Zealand. I haven't a clue what I'll do if I stay, but there's plenty of time to work something out.'

'You'd get a job anywhere. Good plastic surgeons are in demand.'

'Sure.' She didn't want to work anywhere. She wanted to work here. With Tom.

'I can't imagine what it's like to have time on your hands. It's so long since I took a break it's a dream.' Then he lifted his face. His eyes were filled with longing.

She moved without realising what she was doing. She took Tom's hand and placed it on her hip. She tucked her face against his chest.

His chin settled on her head. It felt so right being there, almost a part of him. When he began running his fingers through her hair she smiled and snuggled closer to his lean, muscular body.

She smoothed her palm over his skin, felt the muscles moving under her hand. Then her finger touched a nipple, and Tom's breath hissed through his teeth. Beneath her bottom his thighs tensed. She shifted slightly.

'Don't wriggle,' he begged.

Right. She kissed his stomach. And shifted her backside.

'Fi…'

'Fi, what?' she whispered against his skin, before trailing her tongue up the muscles of his stomach, over his chest to the hollow beneath his jaw. As her tongue found it heat flared between her legs and she trembled. The fire she'd thought she'd extinguished earlier was well and truly roaring.

An icy chill on his back where the bedcovers had ridden down woke Tom. His right arm was crushed under Fiona, his fingers completely numb. Carefully he eased his arm out, not wanting to disturb Fiona as she slept peacefully, her back curved against his belly.

Holding his arm aloft, he opened and shut his fingers, pumping the blood through his veins, urging his cells back to life. Sharp tingling in his muscles caused him to grimace.

But it didn't interrupt his thoughts of Fiona and what they'd shared through the night. Which was a problem. He'd really messed up this time. Not that he'd been coerced into making love with her. No way. He'd wanted it every bit as much as she had.

But it had been a mistake. A monumental mistake. Fiona would be here for another three days. Three days when they'd have to work together, acting as though this hadn't happened.

It had happened. They'd made love twice. And it had been wonderful, fantastic. No denying that. But, wonderful or not, their future had not changed because of it.

Another thought pierced his mind.

They hadn't used any protection. Hadn't even thought about it. His heart-rate slowed. How could he have not thought about it? What if they'd got pregnant?

His heart lurched. He'd love another child, love to be a father again, was even ready for it. But was Fiona? Did she want a baby? *Slow down.* His heart was running away with this. The whole idea was crazy. They weren't getting back together again, so how could he think about children?

The last thing either of them needed was to bring another child into this world. Not with everything that had gone wrong last time. There'd be the constant fear that something would again take away their child. What if he failed Fiona again? It would destroy both of them completely next time.

Slowly, carefully, so as not to wake her, he slid out of the bed and padded across the room, the floor freezing under his warm feet. In his bedroom he tugged on his thick robe before heading for the kitchen, where he switched on the kettle for a cup of coffee. He poked at the embers in the firebox until they were glowing, then added kindling and some pieces of split pine.

If only it were as easy to sort out his life.

CHAPTER ELEVEN

FIONA stretched and rolled over in the narrow bed. She was alone. Some time during the night Tom had left her. The warm, soft feeling inside her evaporated as quickly as the warmth of her skin did when she lifted the covers away.

Had he been called over to the hospital? An emergency? In her heart she knew that hadn't happened. She'd have heard the phone, or someone knocking on the front door outside her bedroom. Over the years spent working overseas she'd always slept with one ear open, alert to anyone needing her medical skills. So how had she missed Tom leaving her bed?

The bedside clock read six-thirty. Time to be getting up and preparing for the day ahead. Groping in the dark, she found the switch for the bedside light and flicked it on, blinking in the sudden yellow light.

Her heart lurched. Across the floor Tom's clothes were intermingled with hers, scattered as they'd hurried to get close to each other. Picking up his shirt, she held it to her face, sniffed in his scent. A lump filled her throat. He'd left her during the night. In her heart of hearts she knew what that meant. Last night had been wonderful. Last night had been a one-off. Last night was not to be repeated.

She suspected that right now he'd be sitting behind his desk in the hospital with screeds of paperwork in front of him. Patient notes, staff rosters, accounts, medical journals—whatever. All to do with his hospital. All keeping him busy and away from her.

This was classic Tom behaviour. Work first, everything and everyone else second.

Disappointment thumped through her head. To think she'd believed they were making progress in reaching an understanding. She couldn't have been further from the truth if she'd tried. They might have made love during the night. It might have been sensational. But it all meant absolutely nothing in the cold half-light of the morning when she found herself alone in his cottage.

Did he think he'd made a mistake coming to her room last night? Was that it? Guilt snagged her. When he'd first knocked on her door he'd said he wanted to explain—and what had she done? Seduced him. He'd made it easy, for sure. But ever since she'd arrived she'd wanted him to talk to her, and when he'd come to do that she'd made love to him instead. The guy couldn't win.

Had he meant to discuss Liam and their defunct marriage with her? She'd been lured into a false sense of expectation when he'd told her about his friend Billy. *That* had been a shock. Now she fully understood why he didn't express his feelings very well. If his parents had refused to listen and repeatedly told him to forget what had happened, then he had no idea of the relief talking about problems could bring. But to have never mentioned the incident at all over the years they were together hurt her. Just as he hadn't once told her about his dreams for a children's hospital.

Shivering in the chilly air, she gathered up her clothes, dressed rapidly, and headed for the kitchen and some warmth. Her heart thumped slowly, painfully, as she tripped down the hall. With each step she reaffirmed what she already knew—the cottage was empty. Tom had gone out. By leaving her to wake up alone he was telling her that they had not rekindled their love but somehow cemented its demise.

The kettle was warm to her shaky touch. So Tom had made himself a drink not long ago. How come she had not woken? Had not felt him leaving her side? She should have sensed his departure. His withdrawal.

If he'd wanted a way to tell her she didn't belong in his life then he'd certainly found it. His lovemaking had been goodbye, not welcome back.

'Hi.' Fiona walked into Tom's office at midday, her chin high and her eyes guarded.

'Finished your round?' he asked, tapping his pen and trying to ignore the tension in his belly wound so tight he felt in danger of springing apart. Where did they go from here? How did they get beyond last night without resorting to platitudes? Or, worse, going back to conversations about the past?

'The ward round was uneventful.' Fiona dropped into a chair and rubbed her eyes. Shadows darkened the skin below them. Her voice drained of all emotion, she added, 'Sophie will be here in a few minutes for her final check-up.'

'Jacob's pleased to be taking her home.' What

he really wanted to say was that last night had been special, but he wasn't sure what the next step was. Six years alone was a long time, and it wasn't easy to suddenly let someone into his space. Especially someone he'd loved as much as he'd loved Fiona. Still loved her.

The pen dropped through his fingers to the desk. How did people start again? Did Fiona even want to? Not once since she'd arrived had she given any indication that she did. But would she?

'I'm sure he is. It has been a long few days for him, too.' Fiona seemed very interested in a spot on the wall behind his head.

Her beautiful face tightened the knot in his stomach and made him forget what they'd just been saying. He searched the top of his desk, saw the file named 'Sophie Clark'. Mentally he banged his head.

'Jacob has been patient with his daughter, letting her vent her distress, understanding her need to fit in with her peers. His love for her shines through even in the most difficult moments.' Tom stood up and reached for a medical book on top of the filing cabinet before adding, 'You helped them both immensely.'

Over the days Fiona had drawn Sophie out of her shell, made her see that a scar did not mean the end of having fun with friends, or being whoever she wanted to be. Fi had shown her own brand of patience; taking her time, knowing when to be gentle, when to put a bit of bite in her words to make Sophie stop and think. It had worked. Anyone only had to look at Sophie to know that. Fiona had put everything into her case and the results were outstanding.

He stopped, his hand holding the book. She'd done that throughout the week with all her patients. She kept trying to do that with him, but he only blocked her. Why wasn't it as easy for him to tell her that by coming here she'd helped him finally come to terms with Liam's death? That he'd missed her and wanted her back in his life? *Why was everything so damned hard?*

Loud knocking at the door jerked his mind back into the real world. Sophie and her dad were here.

'Hi there, Dr Tom, Fiona.' Sophie bounced into the room ahead of her father and dropped onto a chair.

The change from the shy, sad teenager he'd met a few weeks ago still astonished him. While

Sophie's face remained swollen, and the bruising had turned a grey-yellow shade, it wasn't yet apparent how much difference the surgery would make to her appearance.

Sophie babbled on. 'Fiona, I'm going to be a teacher when I've finished school. I just loved looking after those little kids. They're so cute. It's cool fun reading stories and making up games to play with them. And they're so honest. They talk about their scars like there's no big deal.'

Fiona raised a thumb in acknowledgement. 'Aren't they right about that? It's what's on the inside of a person that really counts. All the good stuff. And you've got that in bucketloads.'

Tom tensed. His feelings for Fiona had always been strong. He'd loved her so much. His gaze shifted to her, watched her face become animated as she listened to Sophie's excited chatter. And his heart began breaking again. He still loved Fi just as much as he always had. Maybe even more. How did he convince her to stay and try again? He swallowed. Clenched his hands so that the nails dug into his palms.

And looked up to find Fiona focused on Jacob, who was telling her, 'Much like yourself, Dr Fraser. I want to thank you so much for what you've achieved with my daughter. And I'm not talking about the surgery—although we're very grateful for that, of course.' Jacob's smile could have lit up the whole village.

She looked uncomfortable, being thanked for something she'd trained for and obviously enjoyed doing. All the reward any doctor really wanted had to be the eagerness for life that now glowed in Sophie's eyes. The girl had been through the school of hard knocks and come out the other side.

Fiona washed her hands. 'Let me look at your face before you go. How far are you travelling tonight?'

'Dad's taking me to a posh restaurant in Christchurch and we're going to stay at a big hotel. Then it's all the way back to Timaru tomorrow.'

Tom's attempt at a chuckle missed, big-time. 'A posh restaurant? What happened to fast food?'

'That's where we're really going. Dad's been promising all week.'

Jacob raised an eyebrow. 'Anything for a spot of peace.'

After a quick examination, Fiona told her, 'Time to go home.'

Sophie threw her arms around Fiona and hugged her hard. 'I'm going to miss you. Can I write to you and let you know what everyone at school says about my new scar?'

'Of course you can. Send any mail here, and hopefully the office will know where to send it once I've decided what I'm doing next.'

Tom felt a shard of ice stab his heart. Reality was setting in. The end of the week loomed and so did Fiona's departure.

Sophie grinned. 'Don't you have a cell phone so I can text you?'

Fiona tapped her forehead. 'Duh, I'm always forgetting that I've got one, not having had one while I was overseas. No coverage in most of the places I've been.'

Tom grimaced as he watched his wife write down her number. He didn't want her going back to those places. But it wasn't up to him where she went, what she did.

'Bye, Dr Tom.' Sophie waved from the door.

Returning her wave, Tom slid further down in his chair. Tiredness crept over him. Not the usual raw ache to his body that lack of sleep and too much worry gave him, but a quiet, muscle-numbing tiredness. His eyes sagged shut. Sealing in images of Fi: in his arms last night, operating on a skin graft, laughing and playing lions with the children, crying over Liam's photo.

Her voice came through the images, softly. 'You look exhausted. I'll see you back in surgery.'

As he dragged a hand over his face and sat up, he heard the office door click shut behind her. All he could think was that he wanted her back—so very, very much.

Fiona pushed the front door to the cottage shut and stood listening for any sounds that might indicate Tom had returned home. All day in Theatre he'd been abnormally quiet, preoccupied. Because of her? Last night?

She'd filled in the uncomfortable silence by explaining in depth to Evan the procedures she was performing. It was the second time Evan had come to observe.

Tom hadn't turned up for the game of lions with the little ones. He hadn't been in his office when they'd been called to talk to Shaun's parents about his blood results. She'd had to wing that one alone.

The boy did have an underlying liver problem—one that meant more hospitalisation for the lad.

She'd done her best to cover for Tom, explaining he was tied up with another patient and crossing her fingers that she wouldn't get caught out in her fib.

But Mr and Mrs Elliott had been far too concerned about this new development with their son's health to notice. They'd been stoic in their reaction to the news, almost as though they fully expected bad news all the time. Fiona had wanted to hug them both and tell them that with the right treatment and a lot of patience Shaun would eventually gain good heath. But who was she to make promises like that? Not when she knew intimately how children did die.

Instead she'd told them, 'Shaun is in the best care with Tom as his paediatrician. You'd go a long way to find a better one, and he won't hesitate to bring in the right specialists if they're needed.'

Shaun's father had sagged against his wife momentarily. 'More double shifts at the factory, then. Just as well I work for a very understanding boss.'

'Talk to Tom. He might be able to swing some funding. He understands your situation.' Darn it—so did she.

As she'd left the shaken family a worm of an idea had begun wiggling around her mind. All to do with what she could achieve if she stayed around Hanmer Springs.

First she had to face Tom again. She'd fooled herself into thinking everything would be okay between her and Tom this week, at least as friends, if she gave him a few days to adjust to her presence. She'd really believed that, and after last night her hopes had soared beyond her expectations. But judging by his withdrawal this morning she couldn't have been further from reality if she'd booked a trip to Mars.

Briefly she'd considered trying to find accommodation in the village, so that Tom could have his cottage to himself. But why bother? He spent most of his time at work—nothing new there. If they weren't getting back together then they should finalise their break-up. There would only be the paperwork to do anyway.

Now her fingers shook as she poked at the fire, bringing it back to life in the chilly cottage. Then she plugged in the kettle. It could come to the boil while she took a very hot shower. Later she'd head into the village for a meal. Not that she felt at all hungry, but she had to go through the motions. And give Tom some space.

After her shower she rubbed at her skin with a towel, trying to remove the feel of Tom where he'd touched her last night. As her hand hovered over her stomach her blood slowed. Oh, my goodness! They hadn't used any protection.

How could she have been so stupid? She wasn't on the pill; there'd never been a need. But what about condoms? Surely Tom had some tucked away somewhere? Maybe he didn't. Maybe he'd never needed them.

None of this conjecture changed a thing. They hadn't used protection. Both times. What if—?

Dressed and towelling her hair, she made her way into the kitchen, her mind working overtime as she thought through her change of heart.

She got a shock. At the bench, Tom stirred milk into a cup of coffee. 'Want one?' he asked, without turning round.

When had he arrived?

'Tea, please.' Had it occurred to Tom that they'd been careless last night?

'Thanks for talking to Shaun's parents. I just missed you.'

'No problem. Those two are very strong when it comes to handling bad news.'

'Unfortunately they're getting plenty of practice.'

Staring at the wall opposite her, Fiona spoke softly. 'Have you ever thought what it would be like to have another child?'

He didn't answer.

'Tom? It's just that…well, recently I have.' Very recently. 'I'd love a family of my own. I miss Liam, and I'll never forget him, but I'm ready to have more children.'

'Why are you telling me this?'

Momentarily stuck for words, she toyed with the button on her blouse. Why couldn't he just answer her question?

She knew she'd be leaving soon, that there was no place for her here, so she couldn't waste this opportunity. There wasn't the luxury of time to let Tom get used to having her around.

'We didn't use any protection last night. It's very unlikely that I've conceived—it's the wrong time of the month—but I can't help thinking what if I have?'

Again Tom said nothing.

'If I am pregnant, how would you feel, Tom?'

His eyes met hers, unfathomable, intense. 'I'm not sure. But I do think we'd better hope you're not. Now is *not* the time for us to be bringing a child into the world. Hell, Fiona, we haven't even discussed what we both want in the future, and you're talking about having a baby.'

'The baby thing is pure conjecture at the moment.' She hesitated, suddenly terrified he wouldn't want to be a part of her life again, and yet needing to tell him how she felt towards him. She leapt in before fear could paralyse her completely.

'I came here thinking I'd be able to apologise to you for the terrible way I treated you when I left, and then we could patch up our differences and put the past behind us. I hoped that then we would be able to get on with our lives, knowing that we could bump into each other occasionally and there'd be no bad feelings between us any more. I even presumed we'd discuss a divorce. But being here with you, talking and laughing with you, crying with you, sharing meals, your cottage, making love—Tom, I don't want to go away. Is there any chance we could try again?'

He must be able to hear her heart thudding. They'd hear it in the village. Cold sweat slithered down her spine. She'd blown it. Tom wasn't ready. She'd acted as she'd used to, forcing something on him when he didn't want to hear it. Why hadn't she learned to keep quiet?

Because she loved Tom, and if she didn't tell him he'd never know.

'Fiona, I don't know—'

Wild pounding on the front door startled both of them.

'What the—?' Tom strode down the hall as the door crashed open.

'Tom, where are you? Maddy's had an accident. She fell off the bunk and hit her head. She's unconscious and bleeding. Kerry needs you to come. *Now.*' Craig stood on the doorstep, shaking violently. 'Maddy's bad, Tom.'

Fiona's heart lurched. Oh, no. Not one of the twins. They had to help—now.

All the colour had drained out of Tom's face, but he was already halfway out of the cottage. 'Let's go.'

'I'm coming, too.' Fiona raced out behind the men.

As Tom leapt into the front seat of Craig's vehicle he shouted over his shoulder. 'No! I need you to stay here and cover any calls from the hospital. In case there's an emergency.'

'Right.' She stared after the car's tail-lights, wanting to be in that vehicle with Tom more than anything in the world. To help Maddy, to buoy up Kerry and Craig. To support Tom.

Trudging back inside, she slowly clicked the door shut and made her way through to the kitchen. Fear for Maddy squeezed at her muscles. What if her injuries were so bad she didn't recover? Or worse. Craig and Kerry would be going through sheer hell right now. She knew all about that.

So did Tom. How would he cope? Being there, seeing Maddy injured? Of course his training would kick in, and he'd do everything within his power to save his goddaughter. But afterwards? That was when all the anguish would come pouring through him, tightening his gut, tormenting him.

And there was nothing Fiona could do except sit here and wait, ready to help if called. Would Tom bring Maddy back to the hospital? Or would they go straight to Christchurch and the experts available there? Would they *need* those experts?

She went back to haul open the front door and

peer up at the sky. Stars sparkled at her. At least the helicopter would be able to get through.

Inside, she picked up the phone. She had to know what was happening. She dropped the phone down again and hugged herself tight. A phone call would be a distraction, definitely not welcome. Not even if it was offering Tom comfort. He was with his closest friends. They'd all support each other.

Glaring around the cottage, she battled the loneliness threatening to swallow her. If anything had become obvious by now it was that she didn't belong in Tom's life. He didn't need her.

There—she'd answered her own question. Whether Tom had considered having another child or not, it wasn't going to be with her.

Damn it, she'd basically told him how she felt about having his baby and he'd not said a word. He hadn't taken her in his arms and said that everything would be all right. That they'd work out what to do together if the need arose. He hadn't told her that he wanted a family. Or not.

He hadn't told her anything. *Fiona, I don't know.*

What didn't he know? How to tell her he had no intention of getting back with her? That he never wanted another child? She'd spilled her feelings and got nothing back.

Which left her where, if she turned out to be pregnant? Having only just come round to thinking she'd love a baby, she certainly didn't know what to think about having one on her own. Having a baby automatically included Tom in the picture. But what if he refused to be a part of another child's life? A chill settled over her skin. She wouldn't be able to handle that. She wasn't strong enough on her own. She needed Tom there.

Overhead, the thumping blades of a helicopter broke through her miserable thoughts, and she went to watch it hovering over the village. So Maddy's condition must be really bad. A long, slow breath slid out of her lungs, fogging before her in the cold air.

Please pull through, Maddy. Your mum and dad need you. So does your godfather.

As the helicopter lowered beneath the horizon she decided to go across to the hospital and see if she could find something to do. Anything to keep her mind busy.

But first she left a message on Tom's cell phone.

'Call me at any time of the night to let me know what's happening. I'll be waiting.'

The night crawled by. Fiona tried to push all thoughts out of her mind about what Kerry and Craig must be going through. But the past kept flipping up like cue cards. Liam. Not breathing. His little body too cool. The agony as the truth seeped into her consciousness. He'd gone. For ever. Tom holding her so tight she'd thought her bones would break, and not caring. Her endless tears. Tom's endless tears. Tom trying to soothe her. Tom holding her against him all day, all night. Tom being there for her.

Tom was with Kerry and Craig, fully understanding their terror, their fears, and reliving the past too. She wanted to be with him more than ever.

At six-thirty in the morning she tried his cell phone again.

'Hi, you've reached Tom Saville's phone. Please leave a message and I'll get back to you as soon as I can.'

Click. Why leave yet another message? He hadn't returned any of the previous five calls.

She was driving herself crazy, going over all

this. So she found Liz and did a round of the wards, looking in on all the children. None of them needed her, but it gave her something else to focus on. Then she tried to find something to do in Tom's office. Nothing leapt out at her, and she was reluctant to go through everything on his desk. Down in Theatre everything that could be got ready for the morning's surgery was ready—except they didn't have an anaesthetist. Would that mean cancellations?

'Go to the cottage.' Liz turned her around at the entrance to the medical ward. 'If Tom rings I'll put him through to you there.'

If Tom rings. Reluctantly Fiona trudged through the quiet corridors and then outside. A walk would help. She headed towards the lights of the village. Maybe a very strong coffee would help clear her befuddled brain.

'Maddy's got a fractured skull, a large contusion, and is in a coma. The neurologist has seen her, but at the moment it is a case of wait and see.' Liz was waiting for Fiona when she returned from the village.

Fiona shuddered to think of Kerry's little girl in a coma, with tubes attached everywhere and monitors reading her every heartbeat. 'It's horrible, but at least she's getting the best care.'

'Tom's words exactly.'

Tom had rung at last. And she'd missed him. 'I'll call him back. I need to know about today's surgery list. I presume we're cancelling?'

Liz looked at her, sympathy in her eyes. 'Sorry, Fiona, but Tom said not to phone him. He'll be out of contact for the rest of the morning at least.'

Why? What could he be doing that he wouldn't have time to talk to her? Surely he understood that she needed to know what was going on?

Liz continued. 'Tom got hold of John Newcomb, the anaesthetist who job-shares with Kerry. John's coming up to fill in, but it will be in the afternoon as he's working at a private hospital in Christchurch this morning.'

'Right. Guess I'd better rearrange the schedule.'

Was Tom avoiding her? Pain gripped her. They'd come so close to putting things right, and now she felt as though they were further apart than they'd ever been.

CHAPTER TWELVE

TOM gazed down at Maddy. She looked so fragile, so tiny. But she was obviously a fighter. Against all odds she was still here. Craig and Kerry were going through hell as they watched over their daughter, clinging to one another and to Maddy's sister, unable to voice their worst fears.

He'd finally managed to persuade them to take a break from their vigil and head outside for a few minutes, taking Karla with them. They wouldn't be long; their need to be with Maddy would soon draw them back here. He understood the fear that strangled them, felt the agony that lashed at them.

He leaned over the crib. 'Keep fighting, little one. You're holding a lot of people's happiness in your tiny hands. People who love you.'

He adored his friends and their twins. He'd tried to be strong for them all, had wanted to take some of the pain for them, but knew he couldn't. No one could. The fear that Kerry and

Craig might lose their daughter was as real for him as it was for them. It wasn't his daughter who lay there struggling for her life, but he knew the anguish that would follow if she died.

The little girl's chest rose and fell almost imperceptibly, aided by machines. Her head was swathed in crepe bandages. Her eyes were closed, the skin around them black, as though she'd been punched by a welterweight boxer.

'You can do it, little one.' *Please,* he begged silently.

It was too hideous to think about the consequences of Maddy not making it, and yet he couldn't stop the memories. The pain that never diminished, never disappeared, instead gnawed at him, sliced him into tiny pieces so that he knew he'd never heal. Excruciating pain that got between him and every other thing or person he believed in. It had undermined his confidence, made him feel inadequate as a doctor. Hell, if he couldn't save his own child how could he expect other parents to believe he would look out for theirs?

Yet he had survived. The scars would remain for ever, but they were fading a little. He had gone on to be a good paediatrician, had saved many children from a life of poor health. He'd grown emotionally stronger, having come through the other side of the worst tragedy any parent could think of.

Yes, he'd survived, and he was ready to take another chance. A second chance of family. With Fiona. She was the only woman he wanted as the mother of his children.

What if she had already become pregnant? A long shot, for sure. But if she had then he would be more than happy to be a father again. More than anything he wanted Fiona back in his life, as his wife.

He kissed his fingertips and brushed Maddy's cheek. 'Sleep well, little one.'

He'd been in Christchurch twenty-four hours. As soon as Maddy came round he'd return to Hanmer Springs and Fiona.

On Saturday morning Fiona opened her eyes slowly and peered into the gloom of a new day. Her last day in Hanmer Springs. Three small procedures this morning, held over from yesterday because of their late start, and then she'd be done.

Completely done. With the hospital. With Tom.

He hadn't returned any of her calls, not even when she'd tried to get hold of him late yesterday afternoon. She could take a hint. She'd be on her way as soon as possible.

The cottage felt warmer than usual when she staggered into the hallway. As though someone had recently stoked the fire. Glancing at Tom's bedroom, she frowned. The door was closed. So he had come home. When had he got in? She knew from Liz that he'd still been with Craig and Kerry at ten last night. Again she hadn't heard a thing. But then she'd been exhausted after a sleepless night the night before.

She tapped lightly on Tom's door and, getting no reply, quietly opened it and peeked round. Tom lay sprawled on his back, arms flung wide, dead to the world. Her throat closed around a lump of pain. Shutting the door again, she quickly got ready for surgery, then packed her bags and left them on the floor of her bedroom. She'd collect them later.

Surgery was very quiet that morning—except for John Newcomb. Having been told about Fiona's experiences overseas, the anaesthetist talked incessantly, asking her many questions, which fortunately she didn't seem to have to actually answer.

When Tom hadn't shown up Fiona had sent a message to Evan to see if he could assist. The intern had arrived so quickly she suspected he'd been hanging around waiting to be asked.

Halfway through the last procedure Tom joined them, looking shattered. 'Sorry I'm late, but I forgot to set the alarm.'

As if he needed to come in. She could have managed and he could have got the sleep he so obviously still needed. But she didn't waste time pointing that out. He'd only disagree. 'What's the news on Maddy?'

'She's one very lucky little lady. She's going to make a full recovery.' Over his mask, Tom held her gaze for a long minute.

Relief poured through Fiona. 'Thank goodness for that. Kerry and Craig must be over the moon.'

'Very much.' Tom watched her for a few minutes, then said, 'Looks like you've got everything under control here, so I'll leave you to it. I need to let the staff know about Maddy, and how Kerry and Craig are faring.'

And he was gone, and surgery continued.

Finally Fiona laid down her suture thread for the last time and straightened up. 'There we go. All finished.'

She tossed her scrubs into the laundry basket and flicked the tap on with her elbow. Finished. No more patients to operate on. Her week in Hanmer Springs was over. She leaned her forehead against the cold glass of the mirror hanging over the handbasin. What had she achieved by coming here?

She knew she did not want to leave.

But there was nothing to stay for. Tom had made that obvious. Not once had he returned her phone calls. Not once had he let her know directly how Maddy was doing. She got the news, all right, but it always came through someone else.

Yet he'd looked exhausted and barely able to stand up straight when he'd popped into Theatre earlier. Right now all she wanted to do was give him a massage to ease those knotted back muscles she'd seen pushing against his shirt.

And later? She wanted to be there for him always.

It wasn't to be. She felt sick to the core. She was going to have to start over—again.

She had tried to tell him how much she cared for him, had tried to show him how much she'd changed over the years, but he wasn't seeing her. Or he didn't want to, more like. She had to accept that and somehow say goodbye.

She straightened up. 'I'll go and see Liz. Give her the post-op notes on the morning's cases,' she muttered. 'Then I'll head off quietly, leaving everyone to get on with their jobs. Leaving Tom to do what he loves best—looking after his patients.'

She headed blindly for the door, brushing past two people standing outside talking.

It took Fiona less than five minutes to phone for a taxi, grab her pack and close down her laptop. While she waited for the cab she wandered around the cottage, touching Tom's clothes that were strewn on the end of his bed, picking up his shoes from the lounge and putting them in the wardrobe, rinsing the cup he must have used before coming across to the hospital. She studied the photos she'd first seen on the day she'd arrived. Then went to look at the one of Liam with her and Tom. Her heart squeezed painfully as she placed a kiss on her son's sweet face. Then one on her husband's.

She breathed in, inhaling the scent of Tom and his life. The life he didn't want to share with her. Wheels crunched on the gravel at the front door.

One last look. 'Goodbye, Tom, and good luck.'

Tom left the dining room and went to find Fiona. He knew he'd mishandled the situation. He should have returned her calls. At least one of them anyway. The fact that he didn't want her to hear his anguish in his voice was an excuse. Not a good one. She'd have known how he felt watching his goddaughter struggling for her life.

Why did he find it so hard to just come out and say what he felt? Had he not finally acknowledged to himself that he wanted Fiona back in his life? He needed thumping over the skull with a sledgehammer. He'd missed one opportunity after the other this past week.

'Dr Saville, can we have a word about Shaun's condition?' Shaun's parents stood in front of him. 'We're really worried about these latest results.'

Shaun's mother started crying, and Tom swore under his breath. It wasn't these people's fault that he'd made a hash of his personal life. They were worried sick about their son, and entitled to his attention, but just for once he'd like to ask them to come back later—when he'd sorted his life out. On a long breath he spoke to them. 'Come along to my office and I'll run through everything with you.'

And I'll see Fiona next.

Sounds familiar, mocked a little voice in his head. His jaw ached as he tried to concentrate on listening to the parents' concerns and tried to allay their fears. They had a million questions that went on and on. Why couldn't he focus on them? Because Fiona kept jarring his mind. He had to deal with Mr and Mrs Elliott first, then he'd be free to do what he really wanted to. Find Fiona.

Putting his patients before anyone else again. Putting Fi second.

The words slammed into him. How often had Fiona said that to him in the past? He knew it was true. Work always came first, even when it wasn't urgent.

In the background he heard a vehicle on the drive and glanced out of the window. A taxi slowed, then sped up, heading to his cottage.

His heart banged against his ribs. His mouth dried. No, the taxi *couldn't* stop at the cottage.

It did. The driver got out and picked up a pack from the doorstep, put it in the car. The pack was followed by a laptop and a briefcase.

Fiona was leaving him. His heart stopped. She couldn't. Not now—not without hearing him out.

But she had given him plenty of opportunities. He'd ignored all of them, too caught up in trying to protect his battered heart. Not once had he conceded that Fiona needed a fair hearing.

Fiona clambered into the back of the taxi. She didn't stop to look around at the hospital. She didn't glance up this way to his window. She just went.

That horrible void where his heart should be returned with a crash. Fiona was his soulmate, his best half. What a goddamned idiot he'd been.

So do something. Don't sit on your backside, feeling sorry for yourself. Go after her and get down on your knees and beg her to stay.

With a muttered apology to Shaun's parents he charged out of his office and through the hospital to the cottage. Where had he left the car keys? How long would it take to untie the Cessna and turn over the engine? Where had he put the goddamned keys? Please, if someone was looking out for him at this moment, could they do something to slow Fiona down until he caught up with her? Make it impossible for her to get the pegs the plane was tied to out of the ground, or put grime on the spark plugs so that she'd have to remove them and clean them before the engine would turn over. Anything. Just keep her in Hanmer Springs.

He threw papers off the table onto the floor, searched his windbreaker pockets and tossed the offending garment aside. Where were the damned keys?

Fiona slammed the mallet sideways at the peg in an attempt to loosen it. The frozen ground had a firm grip on all the pegs, but slowly, one by one, she removed them. Her fingers were chilled and she had to keep blowing on them in an attempt to warm them. Who knew where her gloves were? Anyway, the ache from the cold was nothing like the pain squeezing her heart.

She heard a vehicle approaching but didn't stop to see who it could be. No one for her. Tom certainly wouldn't be tracking her down. He'd be in his office working. And now that she'd decided to leave she wanted to get going. *Twang.* The final peg refused to budge. *Twang.* She hit it again. And again. Through her oozing tears she aimed and swung. And missed.

'Don't go, Fi.' Tom's voice. Pleading with her.

Don't go, Fi. Like she really wanted to go. But there was nothing to hang around for. More aborted conversations? Another night of wonderful lovemaking? No, she didn't need those, so it was definitely time to go. She swung the mallet, missed again. If she didn't hit the peg soon she wouldn't be going anywhere. She smudged the tears across her cheeks with the back of her hand before tightening her grip on the mallet.

Two boot-clad feet appeared in her line of vision. She stared at them. Why had he come? Now? When they'd had all week for this?

'Fi, please stay. At least until you've heard me out.'

Her eyes blurred again. She'd been waiting all week to listen to him. 'Why now?'

'Because I've wasted the week and I don't intend letting this last opportunity disappear without telling you how I feel.'

She raised her head to peer up at Tom. 'About?'

'You. Us. Our future.' Fear clouded those grey eyes.

She straightened up. Could she begin to hope they might be able to sort this out? 'Go on.'

He reached for the mallet, gently removed it from her stiff fingers, dropped it on the ground. His eyes never left her face. 'You're needed here.'

She was needed? That was it? Nothing about the two of them getting back together? About how he felt about her? Disappointment gripped her, a tight band around her chest. 'No, Tom, I'm not needed. Sure, I fitted in well for the week, but I suspect no more than any of your visiting specialists. There's no place here for me.' Surprising how calm she sounded, when inside she felt as though she was in a food blender.

'Oh, yes, there is. You bring the place alive in a way no one else does. The hospital has been different all week.'

The blender sped up. 'The hospital needs me. Not you?'

She shook her head and bent to pick up the mallet. This time she hit it square and the peg loosened enough for her to pull it from the ground. 'Find someone else for the role of cheerleader.' She only wanted it if she could have the whole package, and apparently Tom didn't want her.

She tucked the peg under her arm and turned to stow the mallet in the back of the plane. It landed with a loud *thunk*, breaking into the silence drawing out between them. Her teeth bit into her bottom lip and she picked up the rest of the pegs and tossed them in with the mallet. Tom's arrival at the airstrip had rattled her, almost destroying her resolve to leave without making a scene. Not that she'd rant and rave at him. No, she'd more likely spill out all her feelings for him again, and she'd already done that once. Look where that had got her. Some vestige of pride kept her jaws clenched shut. But for how long?

She desperately needed to take off before she said anything, but she still had checks to do yet. No sensible pilot flew without first doing those. The metal screeched as she raised the engine cowling.

Tom came up behind her. '*I* need you.'

'Pardon?' She must've heard wrong. Surely Tom hadn't said he needed her?

His hand touched her shoulder, gently turned her round so she had to look at him. She gasped at the raw pain she saw in his face. What were they doing to each other? She loved him, didn't she? So give him a break, let him tell her what he'd come to say in his own way. Raising a hand, she cupped his cheek briefly. 'Go on.'

'My life doesn't hold a lot of meaning without you in it.'

The tension in her stomach relaxed a little. Hope kicked her heart. But she had to make sure they were on the same wavelength. 'I thought the hospital gave you all the purpose you needed.'

His head moved slowly from side to side. 'I thought so too. At least I pretended it did. But this week, seeing you working with patients, hearing your laughter everywhere I go, your perfume teasing me in the cottage, well—' He shrugged. 'I've been forced to be honest with myself. The hospital means a lot to me, but I can't cuddle up to it in bed at night. I can't share a meal with it at the end of a rough day, or tell it my deepest thoughts. It isn't my wife, Fi. You are. I do need you.' His eyes beseeched her to believe him.

Warmth flooded through her, turning her cheeks pink, curling her toes. She wanted to throw her arms around Tom and never let go. And she almost did. Then… *He hasn't mentioned love.*

Stepping back, she studied him as she absorbed this point. She couldn't, wouldn't, live without love. No matter how much she loved him, he had to love her in return or they'd be back in trouble before the sun set on their first week together. 'I need you, too, Tom, but it isn't enough.'

She turned to tug the oil stick free, inspected the oil level. Perfect.

'Fiona, I know I've let you down all week. You've been trying to talk to me and I've avoided that at all costs. Even telling you about Billy didn't come easily—not after having kept it under wraps all the time I knew you.'

A glance over her shoulder showed him looking so earnest her heart flipped.

'You surprised me with that, for sure.' Warmth crept through her again as she pushed the stick back into place. He had tried to explain his reasons for not sharing his bad experiences with her. Now that he'd done that would he continue to be open and frank with her? The warmth faded. Look how he'd stayed out of contact while he was in Christchurch with Maddy. 'It isn't enough, Tom. Nothing's really changed.' Except her love for him had grown stronger, matured as she'd dealt with their tragedy.

'You're thinking of these past days with Maddy?'

The hope in his voice had been dampened with caution.

'You never returned any of my phone calls. Not one. I knew you'd be having a hard time of it watching Maddy suffer. All I wanted was to talk to you, listen to you—anything that would help you.' And hold him. And kiss the pain away.

'I tried to call you back and tell you how the pain had returned like it had never gone away while I watched the child struggling for her life, to explain how afraid I was for Maddy and her family. But I didn't know how to do it without putting you through all that again. I'm so sorry. I knew you were waiting, wondering, probably feeling the anguish too.'

'You must stop trying to protect me from everything, Tom. I am strong enough to cope, you know.'

'Believe it or not, I know you are. Your strength is one of the things I love about you. It's just so hard not to want to take care of things for you.'

One of the things he loved about her? Hope touched her again. Could they start over? She certainly wanted to, if they could sort everything out that came between them. She tried for a lighter tone. 'Tell me another.'

His eyes widened, and then he grinned at her. 'The fact that you cooked me my favourite meal the other night. You remembered.' Then his grin slipped. 'You seem to have remembered a lot of things about me. The little things that add up to the bigger picture. Thank you. Those things make me feel special again.'

'Tom, you are special.' She gulped. Then went for broke. 'I love you, Tom. I've never stopped loving you, even at the worst moments over the years.'

The thudding of her heart was deafening. If he didn't return the sentiment then she really had to climb aboard the Cessna and fly away. What was he thinking? Would he tell her he loved her? Or break her heart all over again?

Tom's eyes lit up, and his mouth curved into a delicious smile that set the butterflies fluttering in her stomach. She still didn't know what he would say as he stepped up to her and reached for her hands, wrapped them in his large, warm ones. 'I love you with all my heart, Fi. There's never been anyone else for me since the day I first set eyes on you in the children's ward at Auckland Hospital.'

Happiness spread through her like a tornado,

flinging its warm tendrils down to her toes, out to her fingertips, and easing the weight on her heart. 'Thank goodness,' she breathed quietly, and slipped her arms around his neck. 'What took you so long?'

'Sometimes you still are as impatient as ever.'

'Especially when I'm dealing with a certain stubborn man I know.' She brushed his mouth with hers. Suddenly she felt very impatient. 'Where are we going with this? If I stay in Hanmer Springs I've got ideas about what I'll do with my plastic surgery expertise. Ideas that could help fund the hospital, too.'

'You can do whatever you think is best. I just want you back in my life, Fi. That means in every part of it. The hospital, my cottage…my bed.' He kissed the corner of her mouth. 'I'd like to have a family, Fi. With you.'

Fiona's eyes misted over. 'Are you sure? You haven't been able to spare me five minutes most of the week. That's not the sort of marriage I want.' But they were getting darned close.

'I'm absolutely sure. I'm even thinking about getting a manager to take care of all that paper-work I loathe.'

Suddenly she laughed and squeezed him tight. This felt so right. She'd come home. Home to Tom, the man she loved more than life itself. Then they were kissing. And hugging. And kissing some more.

Then just as suddenly she pulled away, looking into those beautiful eyes. 'Tell me again.'

He hauled her back against him. 'I love you, Fiona Saville. Will you marry me?'

She leaned back in his arms, and those swollen lips curved into a wide, heart-stopping smile. 'Shame on you. I'm a married woman.'

EPILOGUE

Two years and nine months later.

FIONA dashed through the gardens towards the new house tucked in amongst the trees and the flowerbeds that Connor's mother tended regularly. She was late.

But she slowed as she came out into the autumn sun. She missed the heat of summer and grabbed whatever sun she could before winter slammed in and created havoc. Freezing cold, icy havoc, that Tom enjoyed and she tolerated. All part of their busy, rich lives—lives they wouldn't change for anything.

Although there was about to be one small change. One Tom knew nothing about yet.

Giggles burst out across the short distance from home and her steps quickened again.

'Mummy, Mummy, here I am. Daddy's been tickling me.'

Fiona reached down and swung her beautiful

two-year-old up into her arms and smothered her with kisses. 'Hello, my birthday girl. Are you ready for your party?'

'No one's here yet. The twins *will* come?' Worry clouded Molly's grey eyes.

'Of course they will.' Maddy and Karla wouldn't miss the party for anything. They adored Molly, had almost adopted her.

Tom stood on the large veranda that ran the length of their new, larger house. 'Come on, you two, stop gossiping. We've got a party to get organised.'

Fiona rolled her eyes at her husband. 'Just what have you been doing all morning if you haven't got everything ready? While I've been working, I might add.'

He grinned at her. 'You can close the plastic surgery unit any time you like, and become a stay-at-home mum.'

'As if.' He knew she loved her work, and enjoyed the fact that the money she made through plastic surgery went towards helping those families who would otherwise struggle to send their children to Tom's hospital. She'd not forgotten Shaun Elliott's parents and the hardship they'd faced to get their son the help he needed.

'The party's ready to go. The barbecue's warming. Just waiting on Kerry and Craig to arrive.' Tom pulled his women in against his chest for a cuddle. 'Molly and I have been having a bit of clean-out of her room.'

'I'm bigger now. I don't want the plastic ducks or the books with no paper.'

The fabric books that Molly had spent hours trying to read. Fiona's heart squeezed. Her baby was growing up fast.

Tom nudged her. 'Thought we could give a box of toys to the kindergarten fundraising stall.'

'Good idea. They'll be grateful for them.'

'And there's the box of baby monitors. All ten of them. I'm sure we could find a home for *them*.'

When they'd learned Fiona had got pregnant that week she'd come to see Tom, Tom had gone shopping for a monitor to put in the crib, ready for the day Molly was born. In an attempt to lighten their fears he'd bought ten. Thankfully not one of them had ever gone off.

'Tom.' Fiona lifted her head, met his steady gaze. 'Don't take those monitors anywhere. We're going to need them.'

He stared at her, his beautiful, strong mouth

curving up into a big smile, the grey of his eyes brightening into a soft ash colour. 'We are?'

'We are. In November.' She stood up on her tiptoes and kissed that smile.

MILLS & BOON PUBLISH EIGHT LARGE PRINT TITLES A MONTH. THESE ARE THE TITLES FOR APRIL 2011.

NAIVE BRIDE, DEFIANT WIFE
Lynne Graham

NICOLO: THE POWERFUL SICILIAN
Sandra Marton

STRANDED, SEDUCED...PREGNANT
Kim Lawrence

SHOCK: ONE-NIGHT HEIR
Melanie Milburne

MISTLETOE AND THE LOST STILETTO
Liz Fielding

ANGEL OF SMOKY HOLLOW
Barbara McMahon

CHRISTMAS AT CANDLEBARK FARM
Michelle Douglas

RESCUED BY HIS CHRISTMAS ANGEL
Cara Colter

MILLS & BOON PUBLISH EIGHT LARGE PRINT TITLES A MONTH. THESE ARE THE TITLES FOR MAY 2011.

HIDDEN MISTRESS, PUBLIC WIFE
Emma Darcy

JORDAN ST CLAIRE: DARK AND DANGEROUS
Carole Mortimer

THE FORBIDDEN INNOCENT
Sharon Kendrick

BOUND TO THE GREEK
Kate Hewitt

WEALTHY AUSTRALIAN, SECRET SON
Margaret Way

A WINTER PROPOSAL
Lucy Gordon

HIS DIAMOND BRIDE
Lucy Gordon

JUGGLING BRIEFCASE & BABY
Jessica Hart